Myth &
Middle-earth

Myth &
Middle-earth

Leslie Ellen Jones

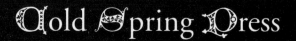
Cold Spring Press

COLD SPRING PRESS
P.O. Box 284, Cold Spring Harbor, NY 11724
E-mail: Jopenroad@aol.com

Library of Congress Control No. 2002108145
ISBN 1-892975-81-5

Printed in the United States of America

Contents

Myth & Middle-earth

Preface

When I started my degree in Folklore and Mythology, J. R. R. Tolkien was one of my role models. I was inspired not so much by his scholarship in Anglo-Saxon as by his fiction: *The Hobbit* (1937) and the three-volume *The Lord of the Rings* (1954-1955). I believed then (and still do) that these stories are an exemplar of how myth should be used to create fiction – not just retelling old tales but writing new stories entirely that packed all the cosmic wallop for modern audiences that mythical narratives held for the ancients.

Much of the richness of Tolkien's Middle-earth comes from its meticulously detailed backstory. The events of the end of the Third Age are the natural outcome of the First and Second Ages, and while the reader of *The Lord of the Rings* may not know much about them beyond what Tolkien chooses to mention in passing or in his appendices, Tolkien himself knew it intimately. Thus, his claim to be writing "history" rather than mere "fiction" has the ring of truth to it.

However, while Tolkien spent nearly twenty years constructing his Middle-earth mythos (he began in 1918, while recovering from the trench fever he caught on the battlefields of World War I), he himself was inspired by the mythologies he had studied, and later taught, at Oxford. The influence of Germanic mythology has been long appreciated, in part because, as Tolkien was an Anglo-Saxonist, it was fairly self-evident. Tolkien was strongly influenced by Celtic mythology as well, however; just as he became fascinated by Germanic myth while studying the languages of Anglo-Saxon, Gothic, and Old Norse, he assimilated Celtic myth through his study of Welsh, the language that underlies his Elvish language Sindarin.

The joy of reading Tolkien lies in the fact that you do not have to know a lot about mythology, or even Middle-earth, to appreciate the story. Those who want to know more about Middle-earth can now read the manuscripts that remained unpublished during his lifetime, such as *The Silmarillion* and *The Book of Lost Tales*, as well as his manuscript drafts published as *The History of Middle-earth*.

Another way to appreciate the depth of Tolkien's work is to explore the mythic themes that inspired him, and that is what I offer in this book. The chapters discuss not only some of the myths, legends, and heroes that inspired Tolkien, but also consider some of the ways in which he modified this traditional material for his own purposes. The choice of topics is to some extent arbitrary, because a thorough analysis would result in a book even longer than *The Lord of the Rings* itself; for similar reasons, I have limited myself to discussing *The Hobbit* and *The Lord of the Rings* rather than wandering into the endless fields of *The Silmarillion*. I have chosen topics that have been relatively unexplored in Tolkien criticism, (although some topics, like the lore of dwarves and dragons, simply cannot be ignored), and I have taken the liberty of giving slightly more emphasis to Tolkien's Celtic inspirations both because they are often overlooked and, as a Celticist myself, I find them particularly interesting.

If I've succeeded in sparking your interest in some of these topics, the chapter on Further Reading offers some suggestions. Welcome to the wonderful world of mythology.

Preliminary Mythological Note

There are many mythologies in pre-Christian Europe which were preserved in some form or another into the literate Christian era. The classical mythologies are those of Greece and Rome, with their pantheons of gods and goddesses: Greek Zeus and Hera versus Roman Jupiter and Juno, Greek Artemis and Roman Diana, Aphrodite and Venus, Hermes and Mercury, and so on. The stories of these deities have been preserved in an enormous quantity of literature – prose and poetry – that was revered in the Middle Ages because of its association with classical philosophy. Indeed, the story of Atlantis, which partly inspired Tolkien's island of Númenor, comes not from a work of "art" but from the dialogs of Plato. The Greek epics of the *Iliad* and *Odyssey*, written by Homer, are very influential sources of classical mythology.

The Germanic mythologies of Northern Europe were Tolkien's official area of expertise. These mythologies are very closely related; in this book, I use the "Germanic" as a blanket term to cover the common themes in the mythologies of the Germans, the Scandinavians, the Icelanders, and the Anglo-Saxons. "Norse" refers to the myths of the Scandinavians and the Icelanders largely preserved in the Eddas: the Poetic or Elder Edda, a collection of poems that contain mythological material, and the Prose, Younger, or Snorri's Edda, a compendium of mythological references compiled by the twelfth century Icelander Snorri Sturluson. Another important source for Germanic mythology is the *Volsungasaga*, a thirteenth century Icelandic saga of the hero Sigurd. Under the name Siegfried, this hero is also the protagonist of the German saga of the Nibelungs. The *Gesta Danorum* of Saxo Grammaticus also contains much about the pagan religion of the Germanic peoples – especially the Scandinavians – though written from a disapprovingly Christian point of view. Anglo-Saxon mythology is closely related to the other Germanic myths, but there is no grand overview of Anglo-Saxon; instead, the mythology must be inferred from references in poems such as *Beowulf.*

There are two main branches of Celtic mythology, the Irish and the Welsh. Irish mythology is usually broken down into three "cycles," the mythological cycle that relates the tales of the Tuatha Dé Danann, the "fairy" or *sídh* (pronounced "shee") folk of Ireland who ruled the island before the Milesians, the ancestors of the current Irish, arrived; the Ulster cycle, whose centerpiece is the *Táin Bó Cuailgne*, the "Cattle Raid of Cooley," and whose chief hero is Cúchulain; and the king cycle, sagas of historical and semi-historical kings into the Christian era. These stories are preserved in a number of medieval manuscripts: the Book of Leinster, the Book of the Dun Cow, the Book of Ballymote, and others.

Welsh mythology is somewhat more sparse; the eleven tales usually published together under the title of the *Mabinogion* consist of the Four Branches of the Mabinogi (Pwyll, Branwen, Manawydan, and Math), three Arthurian romances (Owein, Geraint, and Peredur), the stories of Culhwch and Olwen and of Lludd and Llefelys, and the Dream of Maxen and the Dream of Rhonabwy. The tale of the poet Taliesin is sometimes also included in this collection. The main sources for these stories are two fourteenth century manuscripts, the Red Book of Hergest and the White Book of Rhydderch. (Tolkien's Red Book of Westmarch, in which Bilbo writes his story of the Ring, is a nod to the Welsh Red Book, which also contains numerous historical texts.) There is, in addition, a large quantity of poetry in both Welsh and Irish that contains mythological material.

By the time Middle English was the language of the land, many more manuscripts were being written and many more of them have survived. The main poems that concerned and inspired Tolkien from this phase of the English language are *Sir Gawain and the Green Knight* and *Sir Orfeo*. Although both of these poems were written in English, the critical consensus is that both were strongly influenced by Celtic beliefs and legends about King Arthur, in the case of *Gawain*, and about fairies, in the case of *Orfeo*.

Tolkien also did academic work on the Middle English poems *Pearl* and *Cleanness* and on the handbook for nuns called the *Ancrene Wisse*, but these are not mythological sources for *The Lord of the Rings*.

Of course, in some cases Tolkien took very common mythological themes and made them so completely his own that mythological comparisons tell us very little about what is actually going on in *The Lord of the Rings*. This is, in fact, the case with Tolkien's central theme regarding the Rings of Power. While rings are found as magical objects throughout Germanic, Celtic, and medieval European mythologies, none of them has quite the same function as Sauron's Ring. The practice of giving rings as an indication of a master-vassal relationship was common throughout the Middle Ages and had something of the same symbolism as today's wedding rings. There are cursed rings in Germanic myth, such as the ring that Andvari tries to hold back from Odin and Loki; the gods' insistence on taking that ring leads to the curse on all the dwarf's gold. There is Odin's arm-ring Draupnir, which magically reproduces itself, a ring of constantly increasing wealth. One of the Thirteen Treasures of the Island of Britain is a ring of invisibility owned by the heroine Luned. There are rings that grant wealth and power and rings that attract love. There is King Solomon's ring, which allows the wise king to understand the speech of all parts of the natural world, from birds to animals to plants and trees.

But none of these rings has the corrupting power of Sauron's rings, and especially none of them have the power to grant immortality. Tolkien was right in his denial that he was influenced by Wagner's Ring Cycle; the sources for his One Ring and the other rings of power are too diffuse to be pinned down to a single myth, and his own reworking of the traditional motif too idiosyncratic to make any comparisons particularly relevant.

Abbreviations

In the pages that follow, I use the following abbreviations for the main books cited, followed by the page number in the edition from which I'm quoting. Full bibliographic references are found in Chapter 16, Further Reading.

Books by J.R.R. Tolkien
    H: *The Hobbit, Or, There and Back Again*
    FR: *The Fellowship of the Ring*
    TT: *The Two Towers*
    RK: *The Return of the King*

Books by Other Authors
    Letters: Humphrey Carpenter, ed. *The Letters of J. R. R. Tolkien*
    Road: T. A. Shippey. *The Road to Middle-earth: How J. R. R. Tolkien Created a New Mythology*

1. J.R.R. Tolkien

THE MAN WHO MADE THE MYTH

The man who made the myth – John Ronald Reuel Tolkien – was born in 1892 in Blomfontein, South Africa, and died in Bouremouth, England, at age eighty-one. Over the course of those eight decades, the world changed in almost unimaginable ways. Tolkien was almost twelve years old when the Wright Brothers flew the first heavier-than-air craft in 1903; four years before he died, men had walked on the Moon. He was born in the waning years of the Victorian age and died along with the hippie era. Not only did he fight in the War to End All Wars, he lived through the one after that as well, witnessing the transition from cavalry to atomic bombs. He was born into a world without movies, radio, or television. He saw empires crumble: not only the slow dissolution of the British Empire but the dissection of the Austro-Hungarian and Ottoman empires and the overthrow of Czarist Russia; he also witnessed the rise of communism in Eastern Europe and of fascism in Italy and Germany between the wars.

Yet while the world hurtled forward into the future, embracing modernism and sweeping away the debris of the *ancien régime*, Tolkien stood with his eyes firmly fixed on the past. Not just the recent past, not the world of the Industrial Revolution or even the Age of Enlightenment: Tolkien looked to the Middle Ages, to the era when Northern Europe had only recently turned Christian and people still told stories whose roots reached down to pagan times. Beowulf's battle with Grendel was more interesting to him than the squabbles between the American Eagle and the Russian Bear, even if the latter might end the world with nuclear warfare instead of merely putting a stop to the cannibalization of a minor king's army.

Tolkien spent three-quarters of his life as a professor of Anglo-Saxon at Oxford University, a life that most people idealize as an "ivory tower," removed from the hustle and bustle of the "real world" of politics, sex, manual labor, housekeeping, and balancing the checkbook. All of these things occur in academia, except perhaps the manual labor (although someone who has just lugged twenty-five overdue books from the parking lot on one side of campus to the university library on the other might challenge that). Nonetheless, while the bulk of Tolkien's life was a life of the mind, his early years were challenging and verged on the tragic.

Tolkien was born in South Africa because his father, unable to make enough money in England, had taken a job in the Lloyd's Bank branch in Bloemfontein in order to be able to marry. Arthur Tolkien had loved life in the frontier-town environment of South Africa, but Mabel Suffield, his bride, was less than thrilled with the heat, dust, and petty gossip of colonial life. Furthermore, Arthur showed every sign of having been what in today's world would be called a workaholic; his intentions were good, but every time it seemed he might be able to take a little time off for family affairs, some job-related emergency intervened. For a man of middle-class background and no social connections, he had to prove himself by being the man on the spot at all times.

By the time Ronald (as he was known in the family) was three and his younger brother Hilary was one, Mabel realized that if the Tolkiens and Suffields back in Birmingham, England, were ever going to see the newest additions to the family, she would have to take the boys back for a visit herself. Mabel and the boys sailed in late 1895, with Arthur promising to follow as soon as the latest crisis had been resolved. However, a hemorrhage resulting from an acute bout of rheumatic fever carried him off suddenly in February, 1896.

Mabel was left a widow with only a small pension to support herself and her sons. Both her family and Arthur's had been bankrupted in the boom-and-bust economy of late nineteenth century Britain, and she could not rely on them for anything more than sporadic assistance. More to the point, Mabel was a very independent woman. Before her marriage, Mabel had worked as a governess, she and her sisters had undertaken missionary work in the harem of the Sultan of Zanzibar, and she had sailed to South Africa to marry Arthur completely on her own. She had the emotional resources to be a single mother; money was the problem.

She began by moving out of the city of Birmingham to a village on its outskirts called Sarehole Mill, where she rented a small cottage. The two boys played in the surrounding fields, bothered the miller by horsing around on dangerous equipment, and stole mushrooms from an enraged farmer. Yet, as middle-class urbanites, the Tolkiens never really fitted into local society in an agricultural world of laborers, artisans, and gentry. As the boys grew older, they received their first school lessons from their mother. She taught them to read and do simple arithmetic and introduced them to Latin and French, the standard foreign languages that anyone who hoped to be educated had to know in the nineteenth century.

Ronald was fascinated with languages. Not only did learning to read open up the world of books to him, but he also loved the very structure of language, the differences in pronunciation and vocabulary between his urban relatives and the Warwickshire natives around him, the way adjectives go before the noun in English and after the noun in French, the concepts of declensions and conjugations. What most spoke to him – literally – was the sound of language, its musicality. He also liked the stories you could tell with language. He devoured cowboy-and-Indian adventures of the American West, the folk tales collected in Andrew Lang's Color Fairy anthologies, and the literary fairy tales of George Macdonald and other late Victorian writers. What he especially liked were stories about dragons.

Tolkien always remembered Sarehole Mill as the most idyllic era of his childhood and frankly stated that the Shire and its hobbit inhabitants were based on these golden memories. In 1900, however, things began to change. First of all, he was enrolled in King Edward's School in Birmingham, which his father had attended. Second, his mother converted to Catholicism. In turn-of-the-century England, this was a decision that had enormous social consequences. Catholicism was the religion of the Enemy (an ill-defined Other, French or Spanish or just disturbingly "Continental," an attitude dating back to the religious turmoil of the Tudor era three centuries previously) and of the servant class (many of whom were Irish in those days). It was not the religion of nice, middle-class widows. Respectable people tended to convert in the other direction, toward the more independent-minded Protestant sects of Baptists, Methodists, and Unitarians. Catholicism was viewed with suspicion because its adherents were perceived as giving up their freedom of thought and faith to the dictates of the Pope. The English way of religion was to emphasize the personal, private relationship between the individual and God, not to interpose the mediation of priests and of public ritual.

Whatever financial assistance Mabel had been receiving from her family stopped. Her parents and most of her relatives ceased to speak to her. Mabel decided that it would be best to move back into Birmingham, to be closer to both her new church and Ronald's school. Their first house, however, turned out to be condemned property and they had to move yet again; hardly a propitious return to urban living after the peace and charm of Sarehole. Then Mabel discovered the Birmingham Oratory, a Catholic church founded by John, Cardinal Newman, one of the prime movers in the resurgence of Catholicism in mid-Victorian England; one of the priests attached to the oratory, Father Francis Morgan, became a close family friend.

Father Morgan was part Welsh and part Spanish – his family had made a fortune importing sherry – and he helped Mabel to rent a house owned by the oratory and enroll her sons in the oratory school. Unfortunately, while the house was a great improvement, the school was not, at least for Ronald, who was already showing enormous promise as a scholar. (Hilary was never much of an academic, and after finishing school and serving in World War I, he wound up as the happy owner of a small fruit farm.) Ronald managed to win a scholarship to go back to the academically superior King Edward's School, and after several years of unsettled home, school, and religion, it seemed that the Tolkien family had found their equilibrium.

Stress was taking its toll on Mabel, however. After months of weakness and faintness, she was diagnosed with diabetes. At this time, treatment options for diabetes were almost nonexistent; insulin had not yet been discovered. Within a year, she was dead. For the rest of his life, Tolkien blamed his mother's death on the financial and emotional stress she suffered as a result of her conversion to Catholicism and her consequent rejection by her family. As a result, he regarded his Catholic faith as being as much a sign of loyalty to her as a matter of personal belief. Tolkien may have intuitively hit on the right track: Recent medical research indicates that psychological stress has an enormously deleterious effect on blood sugar levels and can trigger the onset of diabetes in people who already have a genetic predisposition for it.

Ronald and Hilary were thus left orphans at the ages of twelve and ten. Suspicious of her family's intentions regarding her sons' religious affiliation, Mabel had named Father Morgan as their guardian rather than any of their relatives. In many ways, this was a very wise move, as Father Morgan had a substantial fortune of his own and was willing to supplement the boys' meager inheritance in order to give them a decent standard of living. On the other hand, he lived at the Birmingham Oratory and therefore was not able to actually make a home for the boys. It was necessary to find a place for them to board. At first they went to live with an aunt who had recently been widowed and who had no interest in where the Tolkiens went to church. Unfortunately, she turned out to not have much interest in anything; she was, if anything, more numbed by grief than Ronald and Hilary. After nearly three years, Father Morgan finally realized that the boys were not unhappy simply because their mother had died, they were just plain unhappy living with their Aunt Beatrice. He found them rooms in another house, conveniently located near the oratory, run by a Mrs. Faulkener. There was another lodger in the house as well, a young woman two years older than Ronald named Edith Bratt.

Ronald's schooling was going well – after his return to King Edward's, he settled in to become one of the star pupils and he made friends with a cadre of like-minded boys, young men with literary aspirations who were destined to attend university (hardly a sure thing in those days) and who aspired to make names for themselves as poets. Along with three other boys, Tolkien formed the core of a group that called itself the Tea Club, Barrovian Society or T.C.B.S. The name derived from the fact that the group began as a club of senior boys who had responsibility for running the school library and who took advantage of the fact to brew unauthorized tea and nibble on forbidden biscuits. Eventually, the theater of operations was expanded to include the tea room at Barrow's Stores, a department store in the center of Birmingham. Although membership in this informal group fluctuated, the core members of Christopher Wiseman, R. Q. Gilson (the son of King Edward's headmaster), G. B. Smith, and Tolkien himself stuck together even after they finished school, drawn together by their literary and academic ambitions. Tolkien regarded the T.C.B.S. as their own version of the Pre-Raphaelite Brotherhood, the group of artists and poets that included Dante Gabriel Rossetti, Sir Edward Burne-Jones, and William Morris. The T.C.B.S., like King Edward's school, was an by default an all-male group.

Public school education in Britain (what would be called private school in the United States) in the early twentieth century was rooted in a tradition of classical education that emphasized the learning of Latin and Greek and all the things written in those languages: classical literature and philosophy, the history and geography of the ancient world. Over the course of the nineteenth century, the curriculum widened to include more modern history, especially in its political and military aspects (many of the boys in public schools would be going on to become officers in the armed forces), some basic science, useful modern languages such as French, and the important literature of the English language, which at this time was considered to be pretty much limited to Shakespeare and poetry. It was an education aimed at creating gentry: men who could run the government, manage large estates, rule the empire, and chat among themselves.

Tolkien's teachers soon noticed that he had a particular facility for languages. Not only could he learn them relatively easily, he was interested in learning about the history of language, a field of study known as philology. One of his teachers loaned him a grammar of Old English, the language spoken in England from about 600-1100 A.D., and another encouraged him to study general linguistics. A friend who had somehow picked up a copy of a grammar of Gothic, the language of the barbarians who had caused the fall of Rome, sold the book to Tolkien, and thus he began investigating the earliest attested Germanic language. He read translations of epics like the Old English poem *Beowulf* and the Middle English Arthurian romance *Sir Gawain and the Green Knight*.

In contrast to his impeccable public life at school, Ronald Tolkien's private life was, by the standards of the time, bordering on scandalous.

In addition to his tea parties with the boys of the T.C.B.S., he was also frequenting the teashops of Birmingham with Edith Bratt. The friendship between the two began in simple propinquity; Edith and the Tolkien boys conspired to wheedle extra food from the Faulkener's cook, which they hauled up to their rooms through the windows in a basket.

But Ronald and Edith had unhappy childhoods in common as well. Edith was the illegitimate daughter of an upper-middle-class woman who had raised her daughter on her own and encouraged her musical talents, but died before Edith had finished school. In a way, Ronald and Edith's mothers had been similar in their independence and determination to raise their children without masculine assistance. Edith had hoped to become a professional pianist, either playing concerts or giving lessons. However, by the time she met the Tolkiens, her professional chances were fading, and Mrs. Faulkener, who had a reputation for being "musical," turned out to have little patience for listening to her boarder practice scales. Edith must have felt that she was at a loose end, merely marking time while waiting for an uncertain future to materialize. Edith and Ronald apparently spent much of their time over tea sharing their most emotional wounds, and falling in love.

The fact that the two were living under the same roof was the source of possible scandal which caused Father Morgan to separate Ronald from Edith. When rumors of the love affair reached him, he removed the Tolkien boys to another boarding house and forbade Ronald to see Edith. However, since that boarding house was still in the same neighborhood, the two lovers could not help but run into each other occasionally. Ultimately, Edith decided to move to Cheltenham, where she had friends who had offered to take her in, and Father Morgan forbade Ronald to have any contact with her until he had turned twenty-one and was no longer under his guardianship. In the meantime, Ronald had gone to take the entrance exam for

Oxford University and in the *Sturm und Drang* of his emotional life, failed to obtain a scholarship; in his reduced circumstances, he could not afford to attend without this financial aid. All the same, failing the exam on the first sitting was not uncommon, and he could try again the next year.

The second time was the charm, and Tolkien won an exhibition – financial aid worth slightly less than a full scholarship – to Exeter College at Oxford University. He began majoring (or as the British call it, "reading") the classics course, called "Greats." However, after taking his first set of exams, it was clear that his classics, while good, were not outstanding, but his grasp of philology, which he had taken as an elective, was "pure alpha," the best grade possible. His advisors suggested that he switch from classics to English, which was the department that taught philology and all the other ancient languages that so intrigued him, and Tolkien's academic career was set. In addition to the Germanic languages of Old English and Middle English, Gothic, and Old Norse, he also studied Welsh (a language that had intrigued him since before his mother had died) and Finnish (a non-Indo-European language). The latter two languages entranced him with their musicality and became the basis for his two Elvish languages of Sindarin and Quenya. In the process of studying the linguistics of all these languages, Tolkien also read much of their mythology, since often some of the earliest narrative written down in a language is myth.

At 12:01 a.m. on the night of January 3, 1913 – the instant he turned twenty-one – Tolkien wrote to Edith Bratt asking her to marry him. He was shocked to receive a letter in return confessing that she had become engaged to someone else, but the tone of the letter suggested that she had done so because she had given up hope of Tolkien continuing to care for her after so long a separation. He took practically the next train to Cheltenham and convinced her otherwise, and the two became engaged. However, there was now the somewhat contentious matter of religion to consider. Tolkien was adamant that Edith convert to Catholicism, the religion he clung to as much in memory of his mother as out of religious conviction. (In later life Tolkien's Catholicism evolved into much more of an intellectual and spiritual adherence, but at this time of his life it seems to have been primarily an emotional commitment for him.) Edith was not attracted to Catholicism and was apprehensive about the negative consequences of converting; Tolkien, who considered that his mother had been martyred for her faith, was not particularly sympathetic. After a great deal of negotiating and a few major fights, Edith finally converted. And then World War I began.

Tolkien was months from graduating, and while most of his classmates were enlisting with enthusiasm, without regard for the consequences, Tolkien was not as anxious to abandon his potential career and his fiancée. He enrolled in a program that allowed him to finish his degree and train as an officer in the Lancashire Fusiliers at the same time. In March, 1916, Tolkien and Edith were married, and in June, he shipped to France.

Almost immediately his battalion became embroiled in the Battle of the Somme. Gilson and Smith, two of his friends from the T.C.B.S., died in the battle, which stretched from July to November with little military advantage to show for it. Tolkien became inured to the routine of mud, filth, and boredom, interspersed with moments of mud, filth, and terror. The Somme was one of the battles that gave World War I its reputation for criminal mismanagement. Soldiers were sent into battle weighed down with packs overladen with gear that slowed them down and made them targets for snipers. They were assured that the barbed wire that crisscrossed the battlefield had been cut when, in fact, it had been pounded by mortar barrage into an impenetrable hedge that trapped them, to be mowed down by both the enemy and their own short-falling shells. For decades after the war was over, skeletal remains were still turning up in the yearly plowing of farmland that had served as battlefield. The one certain outcome of the war was that it turned much of France and Belgium into a wasteland corrupt with the decay of human flesh.

Tolkien somehow managed to survive the actual engagements that his battalion was sent into, but he fell victim to the other scourge of the war, trench fever. This was an illness transmitted by parasites such as rats and fleas – both endemic in the trenches – which caused bone-rattling fever and tremors, followed by a debilitating lassitude. Those who came down with severe cases could barely summon the energy to move. Tolkien was sent back to England to recuperate in November, 1916, and spent the rest of the war in and out of the hospital. Edith, while glad that her husband had returned in one piece – a rarity in that war, as many survivors still managed to lose a body part or two along the way – eventually became exasperated with following him from one hospital to another, up and down the country. She had also become pregnant with the couple's first child, who was born at the end of 1917.

While recuperating in the hospital, Tolkien began to amuse and distract himself from the horrors he had been through by constructing an imaginary world that he called Middle-earth. In part he was inspired by the artistic aspirations he had shared with his T.C.B.S. friends, feeling compelled by Gilson and Smith's deaths to carry on his art in their memory much as he had felt compelled by his mother's death to carry on in his religion. But he had also just finished four intensive years of studying the languages and mythologies of medieval Northern Europe, and he was now in a position to play with this learning. He had already started developing the languages that became Elvish, a game of constructing secret languages that he had played since his early childhood, and now he took the process one step further to construct a world for those languages to inhabit and a mythology for them to tell.

After the war finally ended and Tolkien was discharged from the army, he and his new family returned to Oxford. He was able to get a job working on the *Oxford English Dictionary*, which at that point was up to "W." He was set the task of not only defining his words but also researching their etymology. In addition, he began picking up work as a tutor for the students who were slowly returning to the university (nearly one third of the students who had been enrolled at the university during the war had been killed). He began to realize that not only was he trained to be a teacher, but he also really liked it and was good at it. When a job in the relatively new English department at the University of Leeds, in Northern England, came up in 1920, he applied. Somewhat to his surprise – for he was still a very young scholar with little reputation – he got the job.

Leeds was good to the Tolkiens. Edith was not particularly happy in Oxford, where she felt out of her intellectual depth. Two more children were born while the family lived in Leeds. Furthermore, after a year or so another member of the English department was hired, E. V. Gordon, whom Tolkien had tutored at Oxford. The two became close friends and collaborated on an edition of the Middle English poem *Sir Gawain and the Green Knight,* which quickly became a standard text for university students studying the language. Tolkien was also given a great deal of latitude by the head of his department, George Gordon (no relation of E. V.), to develop his own curriculum for teaching the "language" side of the department. Tolkien developed a series of courses that emphasized not only the linguistics of the languages, but also reading and appreciating these texts as literature, as stories that had meaning for their audiences and not just as dry treasure-chests of archaic verb forms and references to lost pagan practices, which was the standard approach at the time. In 1924, Tolkien was made a full professor of English Language, one of the youngest professors in Britain. It seemed that Tolkien was set to spend a long and prosperous academic career at Leeds.

In 1925, however, the Rawlinson and Bosworth Professorship of Anglo-Saxon at Oxford came vacant. This was the most prestigious position in Tolkien's field in all of Britain, and given Oxford's reputation, this meant it was one of the most prestigious appointments for an Anglo-Saxonist in the world. Again with little hope of actually getting the job, Tolkien applied; again, much to his surprise (and due to some politicking and a few unexpected turns of events), he got the job. In 1926, Tolkien returned to Oxford, and stayed there for the rest of his professional life. The Tolkien's final child, a daughter, was born three years after they returned to Oxford.

Almost immediately upon his return, Tolkien became engaged in a movement to revise the Oxford English curriculum, much along the lines that he had already established at Leeds. In the course of his lobbying to persuade his colleagues to his point of view, Tolkien made the acquaintance of another new professor and medievalist, Clive Staples Lewis – 'Jack' to his friends. Lewis was not initially in favor of Tolkien's proposal and was somewhat dismissive of the man himself, but the two slowly discovered a shared passion for the literature and mythology of the medieval North and a desire to write fiction, not just scholarship, growing out of it. Neither man cared for the contemporary trend toward "modernism" in art and literature, a movement that had grown out of the cynicism and disillusion fostered by the war (of which Lewis was also a veteran); both reacted to their war experience with a desire to return to the premodern rather than the modern in literature. Lewis also was in the process of questioning his agnosticism, and Tolkien, whose faith was becoming as much of an intellectual as an emotional cornerstone of his life, had hopes of returning his friend to the church. He of course hoped that Lewis would convert to Catholicism, but although Tolkien was instrumental in leading Lewis to an understanding and acceptance of God, Lewis ultimately chose to join the Church of England rather than that of Rome.

Tolkien and Lewis became the focal point of an informal group of friends that called themselves the Inklings, meeting once or twice a week in Lewis's rooms or in a local pub called the Eagle and Child (or more informally, the Bird and Baby) to read aloud works in progress and receive critique from the group. Although the membership varied greatly over time, it was always exclusively male (like the T.C.B.S., which it somewhat resembled); members included Owen Barfield, a London lawyer who wrote several books on the philosophy of Rudolf Steiner; Hugo Dyson, who taught English at Reading University and had been instrumental, along with Tolkien, in convincing Lewis of the truth of Christianity; R. E. Havard, the medical doctor for both the Tolkiens and the Lewises; Warren Lewis, Jack's brother; Charles Williams, who worked at the Oxford University Press and wrote strange, mystical thrillers; and, toward the end, Tolkien's third son, Christopher.

One of the pieces that Tolkien brought to the group was a story he had written down after telling it to his children, which he called *The Hobbit*. The Inklings, especially Lewis, were charmed by it, but Tolkien might never have gotten around to doing anything more with the story had not a friend of a former student, a woman who now worked for the publishing firm of Allen and Unwin, heard about it and asked to see the manuscript. Seeing its potential, she passed it on to her boss, Stanley Unwin, who asked his ten-year-old son Rayner to read it and give his opinion. Rayner Unwin was unequivocally enthusiastic (and in his written report to his father showed an early grasp of the realities of the publishing business, giving not only his professional opinion as a child but also identifying the age group to whom it should be marketed), and the firm approached Tolkien about publication.

The Hobbit was published in September, 1937, and was quickly heralded as a new children's classic. Allen and Unwin were eager to follow up the success with a sequel and asked Tolkien for a "new

Hobbit." Tolkien showed them a number of other children's stories that he had written and illustrated for his family, but none were about hobbits. Then he sent along the massive and disorganized accumulation of pieces about the earlier ages of Middle-earth (material that after Tolkien's death became *The Silmarillion*); Allen and Unwin had no idea what to do with it. It was left that Tolkien would think about a new story – which must contain hobbits! – and get back to them.

He began working, off and on amidst all his other academic commitments, on another story that started and stopped, went in one direction and then screeched to a halt, took up again after a number of months, or years, but slowly congealed as a decidedly darker tale than the lighthearted *Hobbit*. Although he was often concerned that what he was writing was not what Allen and Unwin had in mind, by the beginning of World War II, Tolkien was convinced that what he was writing was what he needed to be writing for his own artistic succor if nothing else. He struggled throughout the war to conclude the tale that grew longer and longer, taking on a life of its own as characters and subplots sprung out of the underbrush of his mind. Finally, in 1949, the manuscript was finished.

Due to a series of misunderstandings, miscommunications, and hurt feelings, it was another five years before *The Lord of the Rings* was finally published. Part of the problem was the sheer size of the work, which Tolkien insisted could not be cut. He made an attempt to get out of his commitment to Allen and Unwin and publish the book with Collins, but then became disillusioned with Collins's plans for the book and had to re-ingratiate himself with Allen and Unwin. The size of the manuscript was a problem, as it was extremely expensive to produce. Finally Allen and Unwin came to an agreement with Tolkien that, rather than establishing a schedule of author's royalties (a percentage of the retail price of each book sold), the publisher and the author would split the profits 50-50; this way Allen and Unwin had a better chance of recouping their production expenses, although, if the books sold very well, they would not make as much profit as they might have under a conventional contract. The first two volumes, *The Fellowship of the Ring* and *The Two Towers*, were published in 1954, but the third volume, *The Return of the King*, was delayed for a year while Tolkien worked on, but failed to produce, appendices with further background on Middle-earth and its languages.

The Lord of the Rings got generally good reviews and seemed set to become a cult favorite. Tolkien, meanwhile, continued his life of teaching and research and often made a desultory start toward compiling and organizing his Silmarillion material. He had became the Merton Professor of Language and Literature in 1945, where he remained until his retirement in 1959. He enjoyed corresponding with his fans, taking great care to explain the personal philosophy underlying his work and its relationship to the mythologies of Europe. By the end of his academic career, his colleagues often suspected that his work on this odd project of his had distracted him from the kind of brilliant publication record usually expected of professors in his position, but he had still produced enough ground-breaking work (particularly his essay on *Beowulf*, "The Monsters and the Critics,") to justify himself, and his reputation as a teacher was outstanding. Furthermore, his influence on the revised English curriculum, which had been adopted in the early 1930's, was a testament to his teaching philosophy that outlived the teacher himself.

In 1965, this quiet life took an unexpected turn. It began because of a loophole in the contract between Tolkien's English and American publishers which allowed a pirated paperback edition of *The Lord of the Rings* to be published in the United States without Tolkien's consent (and without him earning any money from the sales). The American publishers, Houghton Mifflin, did their best to get an authorized paperback version into stores, but because they had to include Tolkien's cut in the retail price, it was more expensive than the pirated Ace Books edition. Tolkien took advantage of the good will he had built up over years of corresponding with his fans to spread the word of his predicament, and a backlash against the Ace edition built up and, more importantly, became news. This inadvertent publicity helped to fuel a tidal wave of interest in the books, and *The Lord of the Rings* became not just a cult classic but a worldwide publishing phenomenon.

Ace may have been somewhat dishonest in bringing out their edition, but their choice of book to pirate was astute, if only in seeing that the time was ripe for Tolkien's kind of fantasy. Middle-earth struck a chord with young baby boomers disenchanted with the Establishment; Sauron and Mordor and the War of the Ring seemed like an appropriate metaphor for the war in Vietnam, and Tolkien's theme of the power of the little guy to effect the downfall of an evil empire echoed the "Power to the People" mentality of the times. Suddenly, Tolkien's unusual revenue-sharing arrangement with Allen and Unwin became the source of unexpected wealth and ease after a lifetime of economic hardship. However, his multitudes of fans also became intrusive in his retiring way of life: He no longer could answer every letter, and phone calls in the middle of the night from fans who did not take time zones into account made his life miserable until he got an unlisted number.

In 1967, the Tolkiens moved to Bournemouth, a seaside resort that Edith loved. She had never been very happy in Oxford, and this move was Tolkien's concession to her now that they had the money to indulge themselves. He continued to putter away at *The Silmarillion*, but the stories had become so dear to his heart that he seems to have succumbed to the common authorial failing of being unwilling to finish a manuscript because he was reluctant to give up the story; the Silmarillion cycle of myth had given his life its purpose since the days of World War I. Edith died in 1971, and Tolkien moved back to rooms at Merton College in Oxford, where he died in 1973. He named his son Christopher his literary executor, and under the younger Tolkien's editorial guidance the mass of manuscripts that his father had left behind were slowly organized and published, offering an increasingly deep background to the four volumes on Middle-earth that Tolkien published during his life.

Although his colleagues may have been nonplussed by Tolkien's literary career – Oxford professors were supposed to write mysteries if they wandered into the realms of genre fiction – his bent for fantasy was not so odd as it may have appeared. Tolkien had become a scholar almost by default. He was good at and interested in languages; he attended a public school that expected its best students to attend university; he did not have any particular talent or passion for commerce or any other type of profession. However, during his school days, his ambitions were all literary. He and his friends envisioned themselves as poets and writers, men with an artistic vision and the passion and commitment to communicate it. Even though Tolkien discovered his talents as a teacher fairly early in his career, when it came to writing, his default setting was always for poetry and fiction.

While as an English professor he claimed to disdain the type of literary criticism that relied on knowledge of an author's life to explain his work (which is a reasonable stance to take when your area of expertise is a corpus of works nearly all written by Anonymous), there are several obvious correlations between Tolkien's life experiences and themes that recur in his work. For instance, both Tolkien's parents and he and Edith were separated in mid-courtship by the intervention of parents or guardians and had to struggle to be reunited, a theme that is echoed in Tolkien's tales of Beren and Lúthien in *The Silmarillion* and Aragorn and Arwen in *The Lord of the Rings*. It is impossible to overlook the similarities between the wastelands that surround Mordor, where Sam Gamgee finds himself enmeshed in the skeletons of long-dead soldiers from the last war, and the desolate battlefields of both world wars.

Likewise, one of Tolkien's aims was to create a mythology for England, a thing he found lacking. The mythologies of Great Britain were segregated by age and ethnicity into the Celtic myths of Wales, Ireland, and Scotland; the echoes of Germanic mythology in poems such as *Beowulf,* which is written in Old English in a single English manuscript but takes place on the Continent; and the Arthurian mythology of the Middle Ages, which spans the Celtic and English-speaking regions of Britain but is also seminal to French and German medieval literature and thus cannot be regarded as purely English.

Creating Middle-earth and its languages was to some extent play for Tolkien, but he also used the understanding of mythology that he gained through his scholarship as the seed and structure for his new mythology. Middle-earth *was* his academic life's work; instead of using his research simply to analyze what had already been written, he used it to write new myths altogether.

2. Philology

LANGUAGE & MYTH

Tolkien proudly called himself a philologist. It is a field of which most people are ignorant today and which was regarded with a certain amount of disdain in his own day, but it had been both popular and fashionable in the nineteenth century. Literally, philology means "love of knowledge." More specifically, the knowledge that it loved was the history and etymology of words.

The discipline can be said to have started at the very end of the eighteenth century, when Sir William Jones, in an address to the Bengal Society of Calcutta in 1786, suggested that Latin, Greek, and Sanskrit all evolved from the same root language, and that the Germanic and Celtic languages probably belonged to this "family" as well. Thus was born the notion of an "Indo-European" family of languages, usually illustrated in genealogical format in the end-papers of dictionaries. More importantly, the comparative study of the Indo-European languages led to the discovery that there were systematic changes that occurred both within a language as it evolved and between languages; the degree of difference between two languages was an indication of how closely or distantly they were related.

This discovery opened up the possibilities for the accurate translation of ancient languages to an unbelievable degree. The problem with many dead languages – those that no longer are spoken – is that there is a very limited amount of written material remaining from them. The smaller the quantity of material, the less likely it is that the meanings of words can be figured out by their context and the fact that there are no living speakers means that you cannot just ask someone what a word means. Once the regular system of sound changes among the Indo-European languages had begun to be worked out, it was possible to look to other, related languages to see whether there were any words there that had evolved from the same root – called cognates, while the set of words that all derived from the same root are called "reflexes" of the root – and to try to figure out the sense of the word you were trying to translate from that.

You cannot simply assume, however, that the meaning of a word in one language is identical to its cognate in another language; it very rarely is. What has to happen is the tracing back, by means of "undoing" the sound shifts that a word can be hypothesized to have undergone, of living words in many languages to hypothetical roots (words and roots that are hypothesized to have existed but are not attested in any writing or speech are preceded by an asterisk); from the many meanings that these cognates have in their languages, a general concept that the root may have expressed is formed.

Thus, as seen in the 1985 *American Heritage Dictionary of Indo-European Roots* by Calvert Watkins, the Indo-European root *gher-¹ occurs in words that have a general meaning of "to grasp or enclose." A hypothesized word from this root, Germanic *ghor-dho-, meaning "an enclosure," develops into the hypothetical Germanic *gardaz and then the attested Old English *geard*, "garden, yard." The compound *midja-gardaz means "middle zone," hence "Earth." Or as Tolkien called it, Middle-earth. Other English words that derive from this root are girdle, girth, yard, garden; Latin *hortus*, from which come the words horticulture and orchard; Latin *cohors*, from which come cohort, court, courteous, and courtesan; and possibly Greek *khoros*, a dancing ground, from which come chorus, choir, and the name of the Greek muse of dancing, Terpsichore.

If you were translating a text in an ancient language that was poorly attested and came across a word that seemed to derive from the root *gher-[1], you might start by looking at other words from that root in the same language and in closely related languages, working back and forth between your own text and related texts. The process is long and arduous, and this was one reason that philology became associated with tedious grind-work. It is a matter of extensive comparison and continual refinement and requires a thorough knowledge of historical changes in the sound systems of many languages. It is also a discipline that relies very heavily on hypothesis and sometimes in almost poetic leaps of faith to grasp the relationships between cognates.

Philology began to fall into disfavor in academia around the end of the nineteenth century as a result of too many leaps of faith that turned out to be not quite so poetically perfect after all. It is easy to see, however, that for Tolkien, enchanted since childhood with the very sound of language, would be attracted to a field that requires developing an almost instinctive ability to understand the sound relationships between words. As T. A. Shippey points out (*Road*, p. 51), the reason Tolkien objected to the copy editors and typesetters who tried to "correct" his spellings of "dwarves" and "elven" to "dwarfs" and "elfin" is that the "v" form is characteristic of an older level of the English language than the "f" form, and by changing his spellings, to his mind, these correctors were denying the antiquity of his creations.

Those poetic leaps of philological faith must be supported by working backwards to prove that they rely on a demonstrable underlying structure. Nearly every book on Tolkien tells the story of how *The Hobbit* had its beginning: Tolkien was correcting exams, and on a blank page he idly wrote the sentence, "In a hole in the ground there lived a hobbit." (H. p.3). His reaction to this sentence was not to keep on writing a story, but to try to figure out where the word "hobbit" came from and what it meant, and in his appendices to *The Lord of the Rings* he finally derived the word from Old English *hol-bytla*, "hole dweller," a word that is not attested in Old English but is entirely plausible and correct in its meaning. This gives an indication of how Tolkien's philological mind worked: He had internalized the structure of Old English so completely and was so steeped in its word-hoard that his brain was capable of creating a completely legitimate new word that was appropriate for its context without his having to consciously think it through. "Hole in the ground" naturally led to "hobbit."

This is much the same process that Tolkien used in creating the languages of Middle-earth, especially the Elvish languages of Quenya and Sindarin. Although Tolkien was professionally married, as it were, to the Germanic languages, especially Old English, there were a couple of non-Germanic languages that he kept as linguistic mistresses on the side: Welsh and Finnish. The attractions of both were, at least initially, the sound and shape of them, the way they looked spelled out on the page and the way they roll off the tongue. Tolkien attempted to teach himself Finnish while he was in college; while he made some headway, he never considered himself particularly fluent, although he was able to work his way through part of the Finnish national epic, the *Kalevala*.

However, Tolkien learned Welsh, especially Middle (medieval) Welsh quite well; he taught the language at Leeds and his scholarship is full of references that show that he was conversant not only with the language but also with its literature. His lecture "English and Welsh" was the first ever given in the O'Donnell lecture series (all of Tolkien's essays referenced in this chapter are collected in his book *The Monsters and the Critics and Other Essays*); academics do not invite someone who is only superficially acquainted with a topic to lecture on the subject, especially to inaugurate an annual lecture series. His lecture, later published in a collection of the O'Donnell lectures in 1963, was delivered the day after the publication of *The Return of the King*, and he begins with a reference to the Celtic influence on *The Lord of the Rings* as a whole. The crux of the lecture is Tolkien's belief that scholars of Old and Middle English must be well-trained in Welsh as well if they are to have any hope of understanding the cultural realities of medieval Britain and its literature. It is somewhat ironic that, while Tolkien's essays on Old English matters have a somewhat dated air today, fighting battles that have long since been resolved, his essay on the relationship of English and Welsh deals with issues that are only now beginning to be addressed.

Essentially, Tolkien borrowed the grammar of Finnish and Welsh for his Elvish languages and entertained himself with the creation of new words, not only their "current" form but also their historical etymologies. The Sindarin inscription on the gate of Moria is a good case in point. It reads: "*Ennyn Durin Atan Moria: pedo mellon a minno. Im Narvi hain echant: Celebrimboro Eregion teithant i thiw hin.*" This translates as "The Doors of Durin Lord of Moria. Speak friend and enter. I Narvi made them. Celebrimbor of Hollin drew these signs." (FR, p. 318)

The imperative verbal ending, seen in *pedo*, "speak," and *minno*, "enter," is *-o*, and both the first and third person past tense ending, seen in *echant*, "made," and *teithant*, "drew," is *-ant*; the imperative ending is the same in Middle Welsh, and *-ant* is the Middle Welsh third person past ending, although not the first person. The Sindarin word for "them" is *hain* and "these" is *hin*, comparable with Middle Welsh *hwn* (pronounced "hoon"). Similarly, the conjunctions *a*, "and" and *o*, "of" as well as the article *i*, "the" are the same as Middle Welsh. If you know Middle Welsh, it is very difficult to read Sindarin and not try to translate it as such.

Here is where Tolkien's invented vocabulary becomes a trap for the unwary. Sometimes the Sindarin words are close to enough to Welsh vocabulary to make some kind of sense, though not in the narrative context. For instance, Glorfindel's greeting to Aragorn on the road to Rivendell, "*Ai na vedui Dúnadan! Mae govannen!*" (FR, p. 222) looks disturbingly like, "It's not a drunken Dúnadan! It's a blacksmith!" Where Sindarin does not correspond grammatically to Welsh is in word order; Welsh is a VSO language (the normal word order is verb-subject-object) as opposed to English, which is SVO (subject-verb-object). Sindarin is somewhat flexible in its word order, but seems to have a bias toward VSO or OVS (object-verb-subject).

Welsh is a Celtic, Indo-European language. Finnish, the basis for Quenya, is not an Indo-European language, whose only European relative is Hungarian. Both Finnish and Hungarian are more broadly related to the Turkic languages of Central Asia. In contrast to the Indo-European languages, which are composed of meaning-elements that are separate words, the Turkic languages are agglutinating languages: The elements like noun, verb, number, and tense are represented by meaning-elements "glued" together into one long, musical word. Quenya is not quite as agglutinating as a real Turkic language, but it does tend to be more agglutinating than Sindarin.

Although Quenya and Sindarin are based on languages that are completely unrelated and have different ways of forming their words, Tolkien related them through their invented vocabularies. Quenya is the older language, spoken by the Elves when they still lived in the Undying Lands, before they came to Middle-earth. Sindarin is a later development of Quenya that arose when a segment of Elves (the Sindar) were separated from other Elves. Thus, the historical relationship between Quenya and Sindarin is much like the relationship between German and English: They share common word-roots but German evolved directly from its Germanic roots while its English offshoot developed idiosyncracies due to interaction with other languages, such as the French of the Norman conquerors of England. As a result, German "*grab*" versus English "grave" shows the same kind of relationship as Quenya *isil* and Sindarin *ithil,* the words for "moon."

The eminent Victorian philologist Max Müller famously stated that "Mythology is a disease of language," meaning that myths are metaphorical explanations of natural occurrences such as the rising of the sun or the boom of thunder and crack of lightning. Tolkien, in his essay "On Fairy-Stories," countered that language is a disease of myth; myth is what is real, and its reality is evident in the words that are used to express it. He responds to a critic of *Beowulf* who complains of the "chaos and unreason" in the poem by pointing out that chaos and unreason are, in fact, the monsters that Beowulf fights, and that those who complain about the fanciful, "superstitious" nature of mythology, in which people fight monsters that do not really exist, have missed the point, which is that chaos is monstrous: hence, stories about the threat of chaos are inhabited by monsters.

The relationships between words – as traced in their linguistic histories – reveal the relationships between the peoples who spoke them and the societies in which they lived. Philologists have tried, for example, to locate the "homeland" of the Indo-Europeans based on the word roots that are common to all Indo-European languages; this is the line of reasoning that has led to the current hypothesis that the Indo-European homeland was somewhere in the Caucasus, possibly the so-called Kurgan culture. As Shippey points out, understanding the relationships between words – especially names – in different languages could elucidate the relationships between history and fiction:

> The *Lex Burgundionum* of King Gundobad opened . . . with a list of royal ancestors, Gibica, Gundomar, Gislaharius, Gundaharius. It took philology to equate nos. 1, 3, and 4 with the Gifica, Gíslhere, and Gúthhere of Old English poems, nos. 1 and 4 with the Gibeche and Gunther of the Germans' epic, the

Nibelungenlied. Simultaneously it became apparent that the epic had a kernel of truth: The Huns *had* wiped out a Burgundian king and army in the 430's (as Gibbon had vaguely noted), some of the names were authentic, there had been a continuing tradition of poetry from fifth to twelfth centuries, even if it had all vanished and never been written down. (*Road*, p. 17)

Philology is constantly engaged in the attempt to prise historical reality from the scattered fragments of words embedded in the poetry and prose of cultures that no longer exist. It is based on the premise that people tell stories about real things, but that there is a gap between the reality and the art; stories are as much about what people think happened as what really happened, about how they cast actions into words that will emphasize their own heroism and their enemies' villainy, about how they frame battle as a reflection of the cosmic order. Words exist in order to express and communicate; therefore, as far as Tolkien was concerned, his invented languages were useless unless there was something for them to say. So he created a world for them to talk about.

Tolkien angrily resisted any attempt to read *The Lord of the Rings* as an allegory. To many people (especially, it would seem, literary critics), allegory and myth are interchangeable terms. In a way, this goes back to Max Müller's "disease of language" comment – he believed that myth *was* allegory, a story in which every element means something else, in consistent, one-to-one relationships. In "The Monsters and the Critics," Tolkien told a story about a man who built a tower out of old stones, which other people came along and took apart as they tried to figure out its "original" source. This was a pure allegory: The tower was *Beowulf*, the man was its author, the people who took it apart, destroying it in the process and then complaining that the tower was in pieces, are the critics. The abstract situation of the state of *Beowulf* scholarship is turned into a narrative that illustrates the conflicts within the field as a "real" series of events. As far as Tolkien was concerned, allegory was useful in certain circumstances to illustrate a point, but it was artificial rather than "art." Myth was real. It was by explaining the innate, transcendent reality of myth to C. S. Lewis that he provided the final element leading to Lewis's reconversion to Christianity.

There have been a number of theoretical approaches to the analysis of myth since the days of Max Müller. Most, however, are based on the philological premise that, as Claude Lévi-Strauss put it in *The Raw and the Cooked*, "myth is structured like language." Therefore, myths should be analyzed like language: compared to their "cognates" in related mythologies, which are then used to suggest meaning, or to fill in "missing pieces," in the hopes of discovering the original myth, or Ur-myth.

Like words, myths are broken down to their constituent pieces and reconstructed; their "grammar" is described. The meaning of names is always important. In the same way that words represent things, mythic images – whether viewed as Jungian archetypes, Freudian symbols, or simply as concretized metaphors – represent the underlying reality that myth expresses. Different schools of thought will differ on what that underlying reality is: ancient, confused memories of historical events and people, the now-lost rituals of a specific religion, the functioning of the human brain through sequences of binary oppositions, the universal struggle for power between parent and child, the quest to distinguish oneself as an individual. Like words, myths have layers of meaning and can change meaning over time.

Lévi-Strauss compared the process of the development of a myth to that of *bricolage*, making something new out of the bits and pieces of other objects already lying around – Tolkien's allegorical tower-builder was, coincidentally, engaged in *bricolage* in this sense.

Creating a mythology for England was Tolkien's goal. Very well. Let us give him the benefit of the doubt and analyze his completed works, *The Hobbit* and *The Lord of the Rings*, as though they actually are mythology, using the tools of the mythologist, looking for comparisons with related mythologies, and searching for mythic themes. Let us see what those bits and pieces of older myths were that Tolkien assembled in his own way, for his own purposes, and how he modified their meanings in the process. This will not completely "explain" Tolkien's work – since he wrote as a modern novelist rather than an archaic bard, there is more room for and also more expectation of personal artistic vision – but if Tolkien truly intended to write myth as well as fiction, it is an aspect of his work that cannot be ignored.

3. The Cosmic Couple

Tom Bombadil, Goldberry, & Celtic Divine Couples

Tom Bombadil was one of Tolkien's earliest narrative creations. He was, in fact, based on a doll (owned by his oldest son, Michael) who wore a blue jacket, yellow boots, and a tall hat with a feather in it. Like many fathers, Tolkien enchanted his children by telling stories about their very own toys — what adventures did they get up to when your back is turned? (Another of Tolkien's children's stories, *Roverandom*, consisted of the adventures of a stuffed dog that Michael had lost on a trip to the beach.)

Bedtime stories slowly evolved into a poem that was published in the *Oxford Magazine* in 1934 called "The Adventures of Tom Bombadil." In this narrative poem, the title character is pulled into the river by Goldberry, the Riverwoman's daughter, gets caught in the bole of Old Man Willow, is dragged into their tunnel by a family of badgers, and finally arrives home to find the Barrow-wight (a malevolent ghost that haunts the burial chambers on the nearby moors) hiding behind his door, threatening to take Tom down into the burial mound with him. All of these adventures, note, involve Tom being dragged down below the earth. Tom banishes the Barrow-wight, then seizes Goldberry from her river pool and takes her home to marry her. The poem ends with Tom chopping willow withys and Goldberry combing her hair: basically, where they sit when Frodo and his friends stumble across them in *The Fellowship of the Ring*.

Tom and Goldberry represent a kind of natural magic in Middle-earth, very different from Gandalf's pyrotechnics and Saruman's technological abominations, even different from the sinister power of the Ring and of Sauron. Tolkien told a correspondent that Bombadil represented the spirit of the vanishing countryside, a kind of *genius loci*, a spirit of a place. Elrond later calls him "Iarwain Ben-adar," which is glossed in Elvish as "old" and "fatherless." However, it is also a Welsh-sounding name that could be playfully etymologized as "hen-seed head-of-birds": *iar* means "hen"; *gwain* means "seed or nut"; *adar* is the plural of *aderyn*, "bird" (in Tolkien's lecture "English and Welsh," *adar* is the first word he mentions in his long list of "pleasurable" Welsh words); and *pen* (whose initial consonant in certain grammatical circumstances is softened to *b*) means "head."

Alternatively, the *-wain* element may be comparable to the second element in the Welsh name Owain, which is derived from either Latin *Eugenius* ("well-born") or Celtic *Esugenus* ("born of the god Esus"), in which case Tom's first name would mean something like "chicken-child." This kind of naming is very typical in the Middle Welsh narratives that Tolkien studied as an undergraduate and taught at Leeds.

But as a Welsh name, Iarwain Ben-adar also gives a hint as to Tom's mythological antecedents. One of the most important early Welsh poets was Taliesin; there are a number of poems that are considered to be, as far as one can tell, the authentic compositions of this seventh-century poet (one is an elegy on Owain, son of Urien Rheged), and then there are a number of later poems of an obscure and mystical bent that are simply ascribed to him because he had developed a reputation as something of a wizard as well as a poet. One of the poems is *Cad Goddeu*, "The Battle of the Trees," which we will look at in connection with the Ents; others proclaim his universal knowledge based on having existed from the dawn of time. He knows because he was there:

> I was with the Lord in the highest point
> When Lucifer fell into the depths of Hell.
> I was carrying my banner before Alexander;
> And I know the names of the stars from the north to the south.
> I was in the Fort of Gwydion in Tetragramaton;
> I was in Canaan when Absalon was killed . . .
> I was three terms in the prison of Arianrhod;
> I was in the Ark with Noah and Alpha;
> I saw the destruction of Sodom and Gomorrah;
> I was in Africa before the building of Rome;
> I came here with the survivors of Troy. *(my translation)*

Now, there is a well-known story about Taliesin's birth: Before he was Taliesin, he was a little boy named Gwion Bach ("Little Divine Poison") who was hired by the witch Ceridwen to keep an eye on a cauldron. After a year of boiling, the cauldron would produce a drop of wisdom that Ceridwen intended to bestow on her unbelievably ugly son in order to compensate for his hideousness. As might be imagined, Gwion Bach happened to be standing next to the cauldron when the drop of wisdom popped out and fell on his hand; he automatically put his hand to his mouth and obtained the wisdom for himself, and the first thing he knew with this wisdom was that Ceridwen was going to kill him. He headed for the hills, pursued by her, and the two shifted shape as the one tried to escape and the other tried to catch.

And in the end, after long pursuing, through various modes, she was so persistent that he was obliged to flee into a barn, where there was a big heap of winnowed grain, where he changed himself into the shape of one of the grains. This is what Ceridwen did: nothing but changing herself into the shape of a black, dock-tailed chicken, as the story shows, and in this shape she swallowed Gwion into her womb, and she had carried him the equivalent of nine months, after which she was delivered of him.

But when she looked on him after his coming into the world, she was not able in her heart to do either of two things: she could not do him bodily harm with her own hand, nor could she tolerate anyone else to do so in front of her. And in the end, she caused him to be put in a coracle or skin bag, which she caused to be watertight above him and below him. She caused the child to be put in this and thrown in the lake, as some of the books show, but others say it was in the river he was thrown, and other say it was in the sea she caused him to be thrown, where he was found a long time after. *(my translation)*

Taliesin is then both chicken-feed and chicken-born, and he is the singer (the sound emerges from the head of birds) who, as Shippey points out of Tom Bombadil (*Road*, p. 97), has the power of true language, in which there is, as a linguist would say, no gap between the signifier and the signified, no difference between the word and the thing, and thus the words he speaks have power over the things to which they refer.

Taliesin is a somewhat grandiose character — he has no compunction about blowing his own horn — while Tom Bombadil is a more retiring fellow. Both share an impish sense of humor, however: Taliesin, for instance, casts a spell so that the pretentious poets in the court of King Maelgwn Gwynedd can do nothing but play their fingers at their lips, going "bleroom, bleroom, bleroom," while Tom flips the Ring in his fingers and peers through it like a peephole, sticks it on the tip of a finger without falling prey to its powers of invisibility, and yet makes the Ring itself seem to disappear. Where the two characters chiefly differ is in their marital status. Taliesin is eternally single; Tom is seemingly eternally married to Goldberry, the Riverwoman's daughter.

Throughout the Celtic world, rivers were associated with goddesses. In fact, many names of European rivers even today derive from the names of their ancient tutelary goddesses: Souconna was the goddess of the Saône, Sequanna of the Seine, Matrona of the Marne; in Ireland, Boand was the goddess of the Boyne, Sinnan the goddess of the Shannon; in Britain, Sabrina goddess of the Severn, Deva goddess of the Dee, Clota goddess of the Clyde. Other goddesses have names that reflect watery associations. Ritona was a goddess of fords at Trier; her name is cognate with the Welsh word for ford, *rhyd*. Although Nantosuelta is usually depicted associated with houses, her name means "winding river." The name of Sulis derives from the Celtic word for sun, but she was the patron goddess of the healing springs at Bath; perhaps her sunny name evoked the heat of the springs.

These goddesses seem generally to be associated with healing and fertility, although a statue of Sequanna discovered at the source of the Seine has the goddess standing in a very cute duck-headed boat, which may imply that she is associated with travel in some way. Likewise, Ritona, as a goddess of fords, would seem to have some power over travel since fords are the places where rivers can be safely crossed. At this time, the main reason that people traveled was to trade, so travel was a thing that merchants did and therefore was connected with wealth. The associations of these deities tended to expand and evolve as the society of the people who worshiped them changed. Fertility was, in general, a good thing marked by abundance, and so the concept of "good" could be represented in a number of ways: many children, heavy crops, cornucopias of fruit, raucous feasting and huge vats of beer, game animals vomiting up streams of coins.

Another common motif in Celtic mythology of the Middle Ages was a woman standing by a river, combing her hair. It occurs so often in Irish myth that it is almost a set-piece; once you have translated one version, all the others are merely a question of small changes of detail: This is the version from *Tochmarc Étaine*, "The Wooing of Etain," translated by T. P. Cross and C. H. Slover:

> There he saw a maiden on the brink of a spring. She held in her hand a comb of silver decorated with gold. Beside her, as for washing, was a basin of silver whereon were chased four golden birds, and there were little bright gems of carbuncle set in the rim of the basin. A cloak pure-purple, hanging in folds around her, and beneath it a mantle with silver borders, and a brooch of gold in the garment over her bosom. A tunic with a long hood about her, and as for it, smooth and glossy. It was made of greenish silk beneath red embroidery of gold, and marvelous bow-pins of silver and gold upon her breasts in the tunic, so that the redness of the gold against the sun in the green silk was clearly visible to the men. Two tresses of golden hair upon her head, and a plaiting of four strands in each tress, and a ball of gold upon the end of each plait. And the maiden was there loosening her hair to wash it . . . . (*Ancient Irish Tales*, p. 83)

Compare this to Tolkien's first description of Goldberry:

> Her long yellow hair rippled down her shoulders; her gown was green, green as young reeds, shot with silver like beads of dew; and her belt was of gold, shaped like a chain of flag-lilies set with pale-blue eyes of forget-me-nots. About her feet in wide vessels of green and blue earthenware, white water-lilies were

floating, so that she seemed to be enthroned in the midst of a pool. (FR, p. 134)

These women are always supernatural in some way, women who come out of the fairy mound or who are fated in some way to go into it; sometimes they are goddesses fallen on hard, Christian times. The other notorious Celtic hair-comber is the banshee, whose name, *bean sídhe*, means "woman of the fairy mound." She combs her hair and laments the imminent death of a member of the family to whom she is attached. In the story *Táin Bó Fróech* ("The Cattle-raid of Fróech") there is a section in which the hero is nearly fatally wounded by the machinations of the evil Ailill and Medb of Connaught, and as his body is being washed, a company of women emerge wailing from the mound of Cruachan. He identifies them as his mother, Bé Find, and the women of his aunt Boand — the river goddess of the Boyne — and they take him into the mound to heal him. The text notes that the women "send forth their wail so that the men who were in the court went head over heels. It is from that that the musicians of Ireland speak of the cry of the banshee." Thus the wailing woman combing her hair is a close relative of the river goddess and the women of the fairy mounds.

Goldberry, then, is the daughter of the river; Tom is the spirit of the land that keeps trying to reclaim him. As a married couple, they bear a strong resemblance to the Celtic tradition of divine couples, found throughout Britain and continental Europe during the age of Roman-Celtic interaction. The Celtic divine couple usually consisted of a Celtic goddess and a Roman god, although pairings of purely Celtic couples also occur; however, Celtic gods are not paired with Roman goddesses. This suggests that the purpose of the pairing was to associate the colonizing Romans with the local goddesses of the land.

A recurring theme in Celtic mythology is the idea that the king of the tribe must be ritually married to the goddess of the land, who represents its sovereignty. When the king and the sovereignty goddess are happily married, cosmic balance reigns. The weather is fine, the crops are good, children are born easily and often, cows give copious amounts of milk, the breezes are mild, and the only war is a certain amount of cattle-raiding, just for the fun of it. When the king is not accepted by the goddess, however, the whole cosmos goes out of whack: hail storms, howling winds, miscarriages in man and beast, invasions by hostile armies and malevolent spirits. The Romans, therefore, utilized this mythological ideology by "marrying" the sovreignty goddess to one of their own gods, usually Mars, Mercury, or Apollo.

The divine couples in Romano-Celtic tradition are usually perceived to be composed of a "god of the tribe" and a "goddess of the land," wedding the human and natural worlds. A good example is the pairing of Mercury, the Roman god of communication and trade, with the Celtic goddess Rosmerta, whose name means "the Great Provider." This pair seems to suggest a union of the man who travels and brings back goods from elsewhere and the woman who tends to the goods produced at home. However, the archetypal "tribal god" in the Romano-Celtic era is some form of Mars, who is the Roman god of war. Roman Mars, though, is a less purely martial deity than Ares, the Greek god who is usually described as his exact counterpart. Mars can be a more protective, defensive god, as opposed to being an aggressive figure who takes the initiative in war, and he has a supplementary aspect as a healer, fixing the wounds he may be responsible for inflicting in other contexts. (Tolkien once wrote an essay on the etymology and mythology of the Celtic healing god Nodens, worshiped at a sanctuary at Lydney Park in Gloucestershire and often associated with Mars in the Romano-Celtic era; the essay was an appendix to the report of the archaeological excavations at

Lydney Park published by R. E. M. Wheeler and T. V. Wheeler in the *Reports of the Society of Antiquaries of London* for 1932.)

One male member of a divine couple who has a Celtic rather than a Roman name is Sucellos, whose names means "the Good Striker," and he is depicted carrying a hammer (an attribute of Norse Thor, who is also associated with Mars). He is coupled with Nantosuelta, the house-goddess with the winding-river name. Another pair is Apollo Grannus and Sirona; here, both deities are associated with healing springs. Sirona's name is etymologically connected with the Celtic word for "star," but her shrines show no celestial associations, being found at healing springs throughout northern France and southern Germany; she is usually found holding symbols of fertility such as eggs, ears of grain, or fruit, and is often accompanied by a snake, a symbol of regeneration, or a dog, an animal associated with healing in Celtic iconography. Apollo Grannus seems to be an instance of a Roman god assimilating the epithet (Grannus) of a pre-existing Celtic god associated with healing springs throughout western Europe. He is often depicted as having solar attributes, and the association of the Roman sun god with the Celtic healing-spring god may be related, as with Sulis at Bath, to the heat of healing springs.

Tom Bombadil and Goldberry do not compare directly with the Celtic divine couples; their similarity to the archetype is on a more abstract level. Most obviously, they are not anyone's "gods," although it could be argued that they are as close as *The Lord of the Rings* comes to representing deities. Tom's immunity to the power of the Ring seems suspiciously deific; at the very least, it shows that he is unaffected by, and thus more powerful than, the magic of Sauron. Tom is a Maia, one of the lesser Valar in Tolkien's hierarchy of Middle-earth beings; Gandalf and Saruman are also Maia, but they seem to be mostly concerned with the doings of the peoples of Middle-earth, while Tom is more concerned with its land. Tolkien repeatedly, in his letters, insists that the Valar, Ainur, and Maiar are comparable to angels rather than gods, although he mentions that denizens of Middle-earth might call on their names the same way a Catholic might invoke a saint's name in a moment of crisis; however, the way Tolkien depicts Tom offers a certain insight into his ideas of how God might work. Tom does not own the wood, water, and land but he is their Master — a word significantly capitalized. Goldberry emphasizes that everything of which he is Master "belongs" to itself; everything has free will. As Shippey points out (*Road*, p. 97), one of Tom's talents is for naming, and when he bestows a name on something, such as the hobbit's ponies, the name sticks.

Mythologically, to name something is often to create it ("In the beginning was the Word," and that Word is a label, a name). Tom "creates" the world and then lets it free, but "chance" brings him on scene to intervene when the small and defenseless (like hobbits) are in danger from the stronger powers of the world.

Goldberry's name seems to refer to the berries of the mistletoe, the plant that was the "golden bough" of the ancients and known to the Celtic druids as "all-heal," *iul-ioc* in Irish Gaelic. (The berries of mistletoe are not gold but white; but the plant is often referred to as "gold-berried," collapsing the plant's two most important symbolic elements.) She evokes in the hobbits a feeling of awe and wonder similar to that evoked by Elves, but somehow more homey. She provides food for the ever-hungry hobbits and she soothes their rattled nerves. She is the one who provides the goods of home while Tom is the one who roams and communicates, like Rosmerta and Mercury. The couple offer the hobbits protection and abundance, guidance and healing.

"Tom Bombadil [is] the spirit of the (vanishing) Oxford and Berkshire countryside," (*Letters*, p. 26) Tolkien asserted in a letter to Stanley Unwin discussing the possibility of making Tom the hero of his *Hobbit* sequel. In a much later letter, Tolkien asserted that Goldberry "represents the actual seasonal changes" in "real river-lands in autumn." (*Letters*, p. 272) Together, they form a classic divine couple in the model of Celtic mythology, husbanding the resources of the land and water, promoting abundance and happiness, and calling the world into existence through the power of pure language.

4. Marching Trees

THE BATTLE OF THE TREES, BIRNAM WOOD, & THE ENTS

In a 1955 letter to the poet W. H. Auden (a big fan of *The Lord of the Rings* who had taken Tolkien's Old English class when an Oxford undergraduate), Tolkien mentioned that the Ents were inspired by his "bitter disappointment" (*Letters*, p. 212) with Shakespeare's depiction of Birnam Wood marching on Dunsinane in his play *The Tragedy of Macbeth*. Tolkien wanted to see actual trees marching on the hapless murderer-king! A bunch of soldiers using tree branches as camouflage was a cheap rationalization as far as he was concerned.

The whole matter of Shakespeare's use and modifications of his sources is beyond our scope here, but it is interesting to note that this motif of Birnam Wood occurs in the so-called "Scottish play." Shakespeare's main source for *Macbeth* — as for so many of his historical plays — was Raphael Holinshed's *Chronicle* (1577). Holinshed says:

> And surely [Macbeth] would have put Macduff to death, except that a certain witch, in whom he had great trust, had told

that he should never be slain by a man born of any woman, nor would he be vanquished until the wood of Birnam came to the castle of Dunsinane. By this prophecy Macbeth put all fear out of his heart, supposing he might do what he would, without any fear of being punished for it, for by the one prophecy he believed it was impossible for any man to vanquish him, and by the other impossible to slay him.

Later, as the end approaches,

Malcolm following hastily after Macbeth, came the night before the battle to Birnam Wood, and when his army had rested a while there to refresh them, he commanded every man to get a bough of some tree or other of that wood in his hand, as big as he might bear, and to march forth with it in such a way that on the next day they might come closely and without being seen in this manner within view of his enemies. On the next day, when Macbeth beheld them coming like this, he first marveled what the matter meant, but in the end remembered that the prophesy which he had heard long before that time, of the coming of Birnam Wood to Dunsinane castle, was likely to be now fulfilled. Nevertheless, he brought his men in order of battle and exhorted them to do valiantly . . . . Macduff [said] . . . "It is true Macbeth, and now shall thine insatiable cruelty have an end, for I am even he that thy wizards have told thee of, who was never borne of my mother, but ripped out of her womb;" thereupon he stepped up to him, and slew him in the place. Then cutting his head from his shoulders, he set it upon a pole, and brought it to Malcolm.

Shakespeare, as we can see here, was not the one who "rational-ized" Birnam Wood; the rationalization was in his source. What is interesting, however, is that the idea of a forest on the march to bring down a tyrannical king seems to echo the idea discussed in the last chapter, that the reign of a good king is marked by calm and prosperity in the natural world, while the reign of an evil king is marked by natural disaster, "prodigies" (unnatural occurrences) and evil omens. The culture of most of Scotland derives directly from Northern Ireland (and, in modern times, vice versa); the early Irish saints' lives and king sagas regard northeastern Ireland and western Scotland as the same culture area, with kings, heroes, and saints traveling easily between the two places and sharing both family ties and mythologies. Therefore, the downfall of the historical Macbeth was very likely preserved as the kind of king saga still found from Ireland about kings of roughly the same era, in which the king's downfall is presented in mythic terms of seemingly impossible-to-fulfill prophecy and marked by the apparent dissolution of the natural world into chaos.

In comparison, let us take a look at the downfall of the legendary Irish king Conaire Mór (pronounced "Connery More"), a king said to have reigned in the first century A.D.; his story was probably first written down in the eighth or ninth century, and the earliest surviving manuscript is from around 1100. Thus, his story was written down during the same general era as the life of the historical Macbeth, who reigned from 1005 to 1034. In *The Destruction of Da Derga's Hostel*, Conaire is the son of a woman born of accidental incest and a man who first flies in the guise of a bird into the tower where she is kept prisoner, then takes off his "bird skin" and rapes her. Conaire becomes king because the druids of Ireland have ritually induced a dream to gain a vision of the next king, and Conaire's father's "bird men" have told Conaire how to fulfill their vision.

The head bird-man gives Conaire a whole list of taboos (*gessa* in Old Irish): he cannot travel in certain directions around specific places, he cannot hunt "the evil beasts of Cerna," he must sleep at Tara, his capital, at least once every nine nights, he cannot sleep in a house from which light can be seen outside after nightfall, "three Reds shall not go before [him] to Red's house," no pillage and plunder may be wrought during his reign, after sunset a single man or a single woman may not enter the house he is in, and he cannot settle any quarrels between two of his slaves. As a result of following these taboos, Ireland was blessed with great abundance, all the people of Ireland were happy and no one committed any murders, and the weather was perfect.

Eventually, however, this idyllic reign shows cracks. Conaire's foster-brothers (a relationship that was often considered to be closer and more binding than biological brotherhood in these tales), steal livestock and forge an alliance with werewolves, breaking the "no pillage or plunder" taboo, and Conaire orders all the miscreants executed except his foster-brothers. The three flee the country and form an alliance with the Briton Ingcel, an equally bad egg, and help him kill his whole family. Then the foster-brothers and Ingcel return to Ireland, to do the same to the foster-brothers' families there.

Meanwhile, having deliberately broken one of his *gessa*, all of Conaire's other *gessa* are inadvertently broken, one after the other, until he and his men are cornered in Da Derga's hostel. In the course of his final battle, Conaire is overcome with a burning thirst, and one of his men, Mac Cecht, leaves the battlefield to find water for him. However, as a sign that Conaire was no longer the land's king, all the waters of Ireland retreat so that mac Cecht cannot get a cup of water for Conaire. When he finally captures a cupful and returns to the hostel, Conaire is already dead and his enemies are in the process of cutting off his head. Mac Cecht not only kills the despoilers and retrieves the head, but he also pours the cup of water down Conaire's headless throat, after which Conaire's decapitated head speaks up and praises Mac Cecht for his loyalty.

Although Conaire's reign is an example of how not to be a good king (or how to stop being a good king), the paradigm of good kingship and its effects can be seen in Aragorn's reign. He is the rightful king, and Middle-earth flourishes under him; on a much more provincial level, the Shire blossoms under the care of Sam Gamgee as its Mayor. In contrast, the lands ruled by Sauron are deserts and wasteland; when he is overthrown (and the rightful king proclaimed), the land begins to return to fruitfulness.

Macbeth's life and death may well have been originally preserved in a saga much like the tale of Conaire Mór. The thematic elements are very similar: a king who is initially beneficent but degrades into tyranny; a set of conditions proclaimed by supernatural figures (the bird-man, the witches) that should keep him in power forever, until the catch is revealed; once one condition is broken, the breaking of the other(s) follows quickly; the king's imminent downfall is presaged by the overthrow of the natural order of things (disappearing waters, marching trees); and finally, decapitation. The rationalizing tendency of Tudor historiography, part of the European intellectual trend toward making strict distinctions between "myth" and "history," euhemerized Macbeth's marching trees into soldiers in camouflage, and as Tolkien noticed, something was lost in the process.

Traditional narratives — myths, legends, and folk tales — are usually composed of elements that folklorists call "motifs." These were defined by Stith Thompson, who compiled the six-volume *Motif-Index of Folk-Literature* (1932-1936), as "the smallest memorable elements of a narrative." Some examples of motifs are motif B11.2.11.2. "Breath of dragon kills men" (like Smaug), or F388. "Fairies depart" (as the Elves depart to the Grey Havens), or F.441.2.3.2. "Tree spirit in elder tree" (like an Ent). Motif scholarship developed out of the earlier recognition that traditional narratives often conformed to "tale types," which Antti Aarne cataloged in *The Types of the Folktale*, enlarged and revised by Stith Thompson in 1961. The archetypal "wonder tale" in Aarne and Thompson's catalog was Type 300, "The Dragon-slayer," which is, in essence, the culmination of

The Hobbit. What became clear as scholars analyzed more deeply the relationship between types and motifs is that groups of motifs can tend to cluster together, but just because they usually cluster does not mean that they must cluster. Especially when the cultural matrix that held those motifs together in that traditional pattern breaks down, the motifs can start to scatter across wider stretches of narratives.

This is what Tolkien has done with the cluster of motifs associated with Macbeth. Part of the story has been attached to Saruman, another powerful figure who starts off with good intentions and becomes corrupted to the point that he arouses the anger of the natural world. Another part, the prophecy element, has been attached to the Witch King of Angmar, the leader of the Nazgûl, who cannot be killed by a man; just as Macduff's cesarian birth circumvents Macbeth's "no man of woman born" prophecy, Éowyn, the warrior woman, and Merry, the hobbit, circumvent the Ringwraith's prophecy. (This Nazgûl, furthermore, parallels Saruman as one of Sauron's dupes and thus can be seen as a kind of double for the wizard.)

Tolkien stated that the Ents, the agents of Saruman's overthrow (or at least the overthrow of Isengard) were partly inspired by a reference in the Old English poem *The Ruin* to the ruins of the Roman baths at Bath as *eald enta geweorc,* "the old work of giants." The poem suggests that the original building, sophisticated beyond the skills of the poet's society, was accomplished by giants, ruined by time; Tolkien turns this suggestion on its head by having his giants (Ents) be the cause of the ruin. In a sense, Tolkien's Ents, as treelike beings, were the means of destruction of the Old English poet's *enta geweorc,* as tree roots number among the forces that will crumble stone buildings that are not properly kept up.

Although the name and the stature of the Ents derive from Old English, and although their existence sprang from Tolkien's dissatisfaction with the Shakespearean representation of Birnam Wood, the final ingredient that seems to contribute to the march of the Ents upon

Isengard is the Old Welsh poem *Cad Goddeu*, "The Battle of the Trees," attributed to the mystical poet Taliesin. *Cad Goddeu* is one of the "nonhistorical" Taliesin poems and is best known as the foundation upon which Robert Graves constructed his theory of poetic myth in *The White Goddess*. There are a number of reasons for taking Graves's theory with large shovelsful of salt as it pertains to Celtic mythology, although as a theory of poetry it certainly proved inspiring to a number of writers. Graves assumes that Taliesin's enigmatic poem refers to trees in the context of the Irish ogham alphabet, a type of writing in which letters are represented by series of notches in different quantities and degrees of angle carved, usually, on the sides of stone pillars or on the edges of sticks. (The stone oghams are all that survive to the present day and they usually serve as grave or possibly boundary markers; medieval texts refer to people cutting oghams in sticks as means of sending messages as well.)

The ogham alphabet is not, however, as archaic as Graves would seem to imply — it appears to have developed under the influence of the Roman alphabet and the earliest surviving inscriptions date from the fourth and fifth centuries A.D. — and so it is hard to accept that it retains knowledge preserved whole from the era of a common Indo-European mythology.

It is true that ogham letters can be named after trees. The alphabet usually begins with the letters b, l, f, s, n, named *beithe* (birch), *luis* (rowan), *fern* (alder), *saile* (willow), and *nin* (nettle). The specific tree names can vary, however, and in addition to the apparently standard tree ogham, the twelfth century *Auraicept na n-Éces* ("Primer for Poets") that preserves the ogham alphabet also illustrates sow ogham (the letters are named for kinds and classes of pigs), river-pool ogham, fortress ogham, bird, color, church, man, woman, agricultural, king, water, dog, ox, cow, blind man, lame, boy, foot, nose, saint, art, and food oghams. While most of these are the basic ogham signs, simply with different names for the letters, some, such as the nose and foot oghams, seem to be a kind of sign language indicated on a part of the body, like baseball signals, and others are illustrated in concentric squares or circles. All in all, the section on the oghams in the *Auraicept* looks like the production of a bunch of monks sitting around the scriptorium with a little too much time on their hands: Hey guys, let's see who can come up with the wackiest alphabet!

On the other hand, *Cad Goddeu* is such an incomprehensible poem that it is hard to rule out any interpretation, no matter how bizarre. The poem represents "Taliesin" at his most cryptic. Again, given that the mythological Taliesin was renowned as a man of unearthly knowledge, it is easy to see how *Cad Goddeu* would come to be ascribed to him: Who can understand it? Must be one of Taliesin's pieces! Graves, it should be noted, was working from the rather unreliable nineteenth century translation by D. W. Nash. Even in a reliable translation such as Pat Ford's (*The Mabinogi and Other Medieval Welsh Tales*), the poem has a superficial intelligibility that rapidly breaks down upon closer inspection. It begins with Taliesin's usual "I have been everywhere and everything; been there, done that" routine, then relates how he witnessed Gwydion, a famous magician of Welsh tradition, transform trees into warriors on the order of God and Christ. The outcome of the battle that ensues is unclear. However, about half of the poem comprises a list of trees and some allusion to how they performed in battle:

> Alder, pre-eminent in lineage, attacked in the beginning;
> Willow and rowan were late to the army;
> Thorny plum was greedy for slaughter;
> Powerful dogwood, resisting prince;
> Rose-trees went against a host in wrath;
> Raspberry bushes performed, did not make an enclosure
> For the protection of life . . . (p. 184-185)

Then the poem returns to another litany of Taliesinic "I was" and "I am"s, "I have seen"s and "I shall"s. The poem ends with an evocation of pagan and Christian, Welsh and Roman authorities:

> Druids, wise ones, prophesy to Arthur;
> There is what is before, they perceive what has been.
> And one occurs in the story of the flood
> And Christ's crucifying and then Doomsday.
> Golden, gold-skinned, I shall deck myself in riches,
> And I shall be in luxury because of the prophecy of Virgil.
> (p. 187)

Whatever *Cad Goddeu* may be about, then, it is linked to both tree-warriors and prophecy. This is what Tolkien wanted to see in the march of Birnam Wood. Is it only a coincidence that this most incomprehensible poem, placed in the mouth of the poet who claims to be able to create reality from his very words, may have resulted in the unhasty-speaking, booming-voiced Ents, whose names are so long because they are the very stories of their lives, always expanding as time proceeds?

The Ents, of course, are not strictly speaking trees; they are tree-herds. But then, the trees of *Cad Goddeu* are not strictly speaking trees, either; they are tree-warriors. The boundary between the herder and the herded is permeable, however. Treebeard comments to Merry and Pippin that many of the Ents seem to be becoming more "treeish" and many of the trees are becoming more "Entish." When this happens, it may be discovered that some trees have evil hearts, or are at least hostile to the mobile species; Old Man Willow appears to be one of these. In *Cad Goddeu*, it is hard to be sure what side the trees are on; they are summoned by Gwydion, but Gwydion is a morally ambiguous character in Welsh mythology. He is a reckless inciter of war and a rapist at one time, a caring and benevolent uncle and foster-father at another; he is both punished for his own transgressions and a punisher of the transgressions of others. The Battle of the Trees is mentioned in the *Trioedd Ynys Prydain*, the Welsh Triads, as one of the "Three Frivolous Battles of the Island of Britain," and the other two are the battles of Arderydd and of Camlann, neither of which is renowned as a noble endeavor with a beneficial outcome. It is interesting that in Tolkien's original drafts of *The Lord of the Rings*, Treebeard began as a hostile and threatening character; what appears to have happened is that as Tolkien began writing the scene, the narrative took off on its own, as stories often do, and the Ents emerged as the champions of the natural world against the (literal) machinations of Saruman.

The Ents' retaliation against Saruman presents readers with a satisfying episode in which the ancient, chthonic powers of the land strike back against the poison and pollution of Saruman's engines of destruction and his genetically engineered half-orcs (bred of Dunlending men and orcs into Uruk-Hai). Like Tom Bombadil, the Ents are husbanders (shepherds) of the forest. Tom and Goldberry seem to live a kind of hunter-gatherer type of existence, picking up what they find in the forest. The story that Treebeard tells the hobbits of the loss of the Entwives shows the Enthusbands as living a pastoral kind of existence, following their "herds," while their wives lived an agricultural life, preferring to plant gardens and stay with them. All are seen as idyllic, golden-age ways of life, compared to Saruman's industrial aspirations: "He has a mind of metal and wheels; and he does not care for growing things . . . ." (TT, p. 76).

Yet this is a very postindustrial point of view. Prior to the burgeoning pollution of the Industrial Revolution, nature was humankind's enemy; it was more powerful than we are. The necessity for the natural world to go out of its way to overthrow a threat from humankind, rather than simply swatting it like a fly (or absent-mindedly burying it under floods, lava flows, landslides, earthquakes, and blizzards) is the sort of thing that would only occur to the kind of person who had had to live in the grime and noise of turn-of-the-century Birmingham after the rural heaven of Sarehole Mill.

The Ents' march on Isengard has a complex origin. Tolkien was inspired both negatively by Macbeth and Birnam Wood and positively by *Cad Goddeu* and the Irish king sagas. Dissatisfied with the first, he dug back into the mythology that probably underlaid the Macbeth story as it reached Shakespeare, and then he allowed that mythology to carry him along and make a point about the destruction of the environment taking place within his lifetime. Tolkien owned a car during the 1930's, but he ultimately got rid of it because he loathed the way that automobiles were transfiguring the countryside, cheapening it and filling it up with "metal and wheels." The Ents are among the most memorable characters of *The Lord of the Rings*, and much of their power derives from Tolkien's masterful reworking of traditional themes and material.

5. Magical Mayhem

GANDALF, MYRDDIN, & THE TRICKSTER

One could make a good argument that Gandalf is ultimately responsible for the entire sequence of events that leads to the end of the Third Age; Aragorn says as much at his coronation as king. Gandalf is the one who decided that Bilbo Baggins would be an effective "burglar" for the dwarves on their quest for the treasure of the Lonely Mountain, thereby both bringing the hobbits to the attention of the wider world and placing Bilbo in the right place at the right time to pick up the Ring. From Bilbo's acquisition of the Ring, Frodo's own quest inevitably follows; it is hard to imagine anyone else succeeding.

Who, exactly, is Gandalf? As many scholars have pointed out, his name, taken from the thirteenth century compendium of Norse mythology compiled in Iceland known as the Poetic or Elder Edda, is really more of a description: it derives from Icelandic *gandr*, "staff" plus *-álfur*, "elf." Thus, it denotes the magical staff carried by a wizard, and indeed, Gandalf is invariably depicted carrying a staff with which he performs his pyrotechnics. Gandalf is merely one of his names, however; he is known to the Elves as Mithrandir (the Grey Pilgrim), Tharkûn to the dwarves, Incánus to the Haradrim, and in his original form as a Maia his name was Olórin. Not only his name but his nature appears to change with each beholder. The hobbits regard him as a jolly entertainer, a figure whose fireworks and stories make him a welcome and legendary guest. The Elves have a more accurate assessment of the nature of his magical powers and his true mission in Middle-earth. The dwarves appear to respect him as a source of knowledge, but they are less attuned to his higher calling. The Men of Middle-earth are, with the exception of the Dúnedain, suspicious of him: he is too talented, too tricky, too apt to come out on top of whatever situation he pops into to be truly trustworthy. He wears one of the three Elven rings, the only rings that are able to repulse Sauron's attempts to control their wearers.

Even when Gandalf seems to be pinned down, his true powers revealed and his character, in a moment of crisis, exposed on the bridge of Khazad-dûm, he transcends physical death and is "reborn" as Gandalf the White, rather than Gandalf the Grey. He is a mercurial figure in every sense of the word. Like the god Mercury, Gandalf is a traveler. Mercury was the patron of thieves; Gandalf a provider of burglers. They even dress alike. Mercury wore a cloak, a winged hat, and winged sandals, and carried a staff; Gandalf wears a cloak, a floppy hat, boots, and carries a staff.

Although Tolkien's readers are always certain that Gandalf is one of the good guys, the Men of Middle-earth, especially the Rohirrim, are less sure. To them, he appears somewhat closer to the Norse trickster-god Loki, an ill-tempered troublemaker who is responsible for the death of Baldr the Beautiful, and whose writhings under his punishment for that murder are the cause of earthquakes. However, Loki is associated with fire and magic, like Gandalf the wizard and fireworks master. He is also a character who likes to set events in motion and then watch as others carry out his work; although less malicious than Loki and with better cause, Gandalf also often sets events in motion (as when he introduces Bilbo into the dwarves' quest) and departs to allow events to follow their course without him.

Odin is another god who seems to have influenced Tolkien's depiction of Gandalf. Odin is not only the chief god of the Northmen, he is also their most powerful magician. He, too, travels incognito, wrapped up in a cloak with a hood or hat hiding his face, and he has a magic, fast-running horse (with eight legs) named Sleipnir. Odin is also the god who leads warriors in battle — the berserkers, who transform into bear shape in their battle-frenzy and have dedicated themselves to him (shades of the relationship between Gandalf and Beorn) — and he sends his Valkyries to bring those who die in the battle to feast in Valhalla until the end of time. Here Odin offers a model for the Gandalf who leads the men of Minas Tirith in the Battle of the Pelennor Fields.

Gandalf's closest mythological counterpart, however, is the magician Merlin, known in Welsh as Myrddin (pronounced "Murthe-in"). Merlin is best known as King Arthur's wizard, and popular conceptions of him are much affected by the absent-minded, backwards-living greybeard of *The Sword in the Stone* (in both T. H. White's 1938 novel and the 1963 Disney animated movie), the sharp, slightly mad druid/wizard played by Nicol Williamson in John Boorman's movie *Excalibur* (1981), or the stately counselor and doomed, doting lover of Victorian poetry, especially of Alfred, Lord Tennyson's *Idylls of the King* (1859). The Welsh Myrddin was probably closest to the *Excalibur* Merlin, but still not identical. He went mad in the Battle of Arderydd (one of the *other* Three Frivolous Battles mentioned in Chapter 4, along with the Battle of the Trees, *Cad Goddeu*) and thus is known as Myrddin Wyllt, "Wild (or Mad) Merlin." He lived in the forest of Celyddon in the western lowlands of Scotland, hiding in terror from the king Rhydderch Hael of Strathclyde, who had killed Myrddin's lord, Gwenddoleu, in that battle. Like Taliesin, whom he somewhat resembles, Myrddin was said to have uttered prophetic poetry from his forest lair.

This Myrddin Wyllt overlaps in many ways with two other Celtic figures, the Irish Suibhne Geilt (Mad Sweeney), a king who also went mad in battle, this time as the result of a saint's curse, and the Scottish Lailoken, a mad prophet associated with that same King Rhydderch Hael who is Myrddin's nemesis. All three are said to have died through a combination of circumstances so that it cannot be said that he died of a single one of them — transfixed by a spear and thereby pitching forward into some kind of liquid in which they drown.

Nikolai Tolstoy, in *The Quest for Merlin* (1985), has argued that these deaths are faint echoes of the Indo-European motif of the threefold death, in which a god is killed/sacrificed by being simultaneously hanged, stabbed, and drowned. He also connects the figures of Myrddin, Suibhne, and Lailoken with the Celtic god Lug (who in his Welsh incarnation as Lleu is killed by being pierced with a spear while standing on the edge of a bathtub, transforms into an eagle, and is discovered at the top of what seems to be a World Tree) as well as the Norse god Odin (who "sacrifices himself to himself," hanging from the World Tree, wounded by a spear, for nine days and nine nights in order to acquire the mead of poetry, a story that contains echoes and parallels to the story of Gwion Bach's acquisition of poetic knowledge and transformation into Taliesin). Both Lug and Odin are connected, by classical commentators, with the Roman god Mercury. (There are times when Northern European mythology begins to resemble life in a very small town — everyone is related to everyone else, and you keep running into them over and over.)

It is not particularly clear how the Welsh poet-warrior Myrddin — who, if he had any historical reality, went mad in A.D. 573 in southern Scotland — became associated as Merlin with the legendary King Arthur who, if he had any historical reality, lived at least a century earlier. Arthur is a figure associated with the interim between the cessation of Roman government in their colony of Britannia in the middle of the fifth century and the serious influx of the Germanic Angles, Saxons, and Jutes by the beginning of the sixth. (It is most likely that the change of his name from "Myrddin" to "Merlin" took place under the influence of the Norman conquerors of Britain, in whose French tongue the name "Myrddin" sounded a little too close to their word "merde.") The relationship of king and magical advisor that evolved between Arthur and Merlin in the medieval Arthurian romances is the paradigm that Tolkien follows in depicting the relationship between Aragorn and Gandalf. Like Merlin, Gandalf advises the king-to-be and assists him in battle, but he also disappears to allow the king to take charge and prove himself in trying circumstances.

By the time Geoffrey of Monmouth wrote his legendary *Historia Regum Britanniae* (The History of the Kings of Britain), which was completed around 1136, it would appear that Merlin and Arthur were already associated in his sources. Not too closely or irrevocably associated, however, because after completing that work, someone apparently brought to Geoffrey's attention the body of Welsh poetry ascribed to Myrddin, which he then constructed into the *Vita Merlini* (Life of Merlin), completed in 1150, which does not synthesize with the Merlin presented in the *Historia* very well.

The Merlin of the *Historia* is initially introduced as a sacrificial victim (like Odin or Lug). Vortigern, the weak and tyrannical ruler of Britain who is responsible for inviting the Saxons to come over as mercenaries, wants to build a stronghold in Snowdonia, but his fortress keeps falling down. His (druidic?) advisors tell him he must sacrifice a boy not born of a human father, whose blood will keep the foundations stable. Such a boy is discovered — he is the offspring of a nun and a demon — and brought to Vortigern, but the boy, Merlin, tells the king that his advisors are mistaken; his blood will not stabilize the foundations of Vortigern's castle, but his wisdom will. There are two dragons buried on the site, whose thrashings are causing the fortress to fall. (This motif of the potential sacrificial victim who knows the real solution to the king's problem also occurs in the Irish story of "The Adventure of Art, son of Conn," while the motif of the hidden dragons occurs in the Welsh tale of "Lludd and Llefelys," and the notion of a supernatural thrashing about causing the earth to shake is, as we have seen, associated with the Scandinavian Loki.)

Merlin not only solved Vortigern's problems, he also pronounced a series of prophecies; after Vortigern was overthrown by the more noble and nationalistic Aurelius, Merlin imported the stone circle called the "Giant's Dance" from Ireland and set it up on Salisbury Plain as a monument to the warriors who had died defending their land from the Saxons. Thus, Stonehenge. Geoffrey relates Merlin's role in transforming Uther Pendragon into the likeness of Gorlois of Cornwall in order to beget Arthur on Ygerna, but after this Merlin drops out of the story. In Geoffrey's work, Merlin is an advisor to Arthur's three predecessors, not to the great king himself.

Merlin's intervention in Arthur's life begins in the poem *Merlin* by the Burgundian Robert de Boron, written around 1200. De Boron also introduces the themes of Merlin's fondness for shape-shifting and other tricks, which may reflect a conflation of the Welsh figures of Myrddin and the shape-shifting Taliesin. Merlin is also noted for his sardonic laughter at moments when he sees more deeply and truly what is happening around him than the superficial social facades by which people hope to present their best faces. This habit of sardonic laughter, allusive speech, and supernatural insight may also be a faint echo of the source of all medieval Welsh wizards: the pre-Christian Celtic druidic order. De Boron's poem is incomplete, and it is in a continuation called the *Suite du Merlin* or the *Huth Merlin*, written by an anonymous thirteenth century author, that the story of Merlin's enchantment by his duplicitous lover Nimue or Viviane is told. This enchantress inveigled Merlin's magical secrets from him and then imprisoned him in or under a stone, cave, or glass tower, from which he can never be freed, but within which he will never die.

As Nikolai Tolstoy has pointed out in *The Quest for Merlin*, Gandalf and Merlin share characteristics of magic, wisdom, power, and especially humor; both have a habit of leaving their charges to deal with adventure themselves but nonetheless appear out of the blue to save the day when really needed. Both are also fond of disguising themselves as beggars or wanderers and of exhibiting their pyrotechnic skills.

The underlying archetype that unites all these figures — Gandalf, Loki, Odin, Myrddin, Suibhne, Lailoken, and Merlin — is the trickster. This mythological figure has many aspects and can appear in both myth and literature to greater or lesser degrees and intensities. Some cultures have deities, such as the Yoruba god Legba or the Greek Hermes, whose whole purpose is to be a trickster; some gods and many legendary or fictional characters are merely trickster-ish, sometimes behaving like a trickster, but having other characteristics and functions as well. The more a literature is subject to the standards of realism, the less purely tricksterish a character can really be — shapeshifting becomes a fondness for acting and disguise, real magic becomes legerdemain. Sherlock Holmes is a good example of a modern modification of the trickster. Tricksters are mercurial, a word derived from the name of the Roman trickster god Mercury.

The kinds of "tricks" a trickster plays vary across cultures. Some mythological figures, such as the Winnebago trickster Wakdjungkaga, are cosmogonic (world-creating) figures, but the benefits they create for humankind occur almost by accident and the trickster is usually involved in some kind of sexual or scatological mishap in the process. This is because tricksters are agents of chaos, and what they create occurs as the result of the breaking down of old structures so that something new has the mythological room to be created. Yet, being creatures of chaos, tricksters can understand and interpret chaos;

again, Sherlock Holmes, the archetypal detective, uses his tricksterish mentality to understand the truth behind seemingly chaotic crime scenes.

On the whole, as William J. Hynes as summarized the figure in a 1993 essay in *Mythical Trickster Figures*, tricksters are ambiguous and anomalous, deceivers and trick-players, shape-shifters, situation-inverters, messengers and imitators of the gods, and sacred and lewd bricoleurs (the French for a person who makes new objects out of bits and pieces of old objects that are just sitting around the place, taken out of their original context, and put to new use; as mentioned in chapter 2, the mythologist Claude Lévi-Strauss adopted the word to describe the way that he believed myths were constructed.) Barbara Babcock-Abrahams describes the trickster as creating "a tolerated margin of mess;" Laura Makarius calls the trickster "the necessary breaker of taboos." One way in which tricksters are universal yet culturally specific is that they are almost always notable for their speech but, for instance, some tricksters are extraordinarily glib while others may lisp or stutter. What is consistent is that they rarely speak normally; their speech is "marked" as being in some way anomalous.

In the Northern European mythologies that influenced Tolkien, trickster figures are often associated with poetry, a kind of "marked" speech. As with the biblical statement that "In the beginning was the Word," poetic, marked words are a means of creating order out of chaos. This quality is seen as magical, and thus Northern European tricksters are also often wizards, magicians, or sorcerers. Consider Gandalf in the context of the trickster traits enumerated above:

Ambiguous and anomalous: Gandalf, as a Maia, is anomalous among the peoples of Middle-earth, and he often speaks in an allusive manner incomprehensible to his hobbitish audience and must be prodded to explain himself.

Deceiver and trick-player: Gandalf is not particularly deceptive, but the magic and fireworks for which he is known in the Shire are

entertaining "tricks," and the Rohirrim clearly regard his appropria-
tion of Shadowfax as a trick and consider him as deceptive (until he
reveals that it is Wormtongue who is the real deceiver).

Shape-shifter. Gandalf returns from the abyss as White rather than
Grey, and while he does not literally turn into a completely different
form as, say, Beorn does in *The Hobbit,* he does have a tendency to be
suddenly seen in a new light, much taller and more powerful than the
hobbits usually perceive him, and then return to good old Gandalf (for
instance, when he has to threaten Bilbo to leave the Ring behind for
Frodo at the very beginning of *The Fellowship of the Ring*).

Situation-inverter. Most memorably, Gandalf turns the cozy,
provincial, comfort-loving Bilbo Baggins into a professional burglar
and adventurer, but his interventions in almost every case turn things
on their heads, luckily for the better in the case of Our Heroes.

Messenger and imitator of the gods: Tolkien describes the Maiar,
such as Gandalf, as being the Middle-earth equivalents of angels, and
the very word "angel" means "messenger of God."

Sacred and lewd bricoleur. As so many commentators have noted,
there is nothing lewd in Tolkien, ever; however, in a very real sense,
Gandalf acts as a sacred bricoleur using actual individuals as his
creative materials, constructing not only the dwarf party in *The
Hobbit* but also the Fellowship in *The Lord of the Rings* out of the
individuals at hand to set in play the forces that will eventually bring
the Third Age to a generally beneficial end (Sauron defeated, good;
loss of Elves, sad).

Judeo-Christian theology is not particularly conducive to
tricksterism, although tricksters pop up, irrepressible, in many aspects
of popular Jewish and Christian tradition, often as saints (miracle-
working is a tricksterish trait), invariably within the oral tradition.
The God of the Book, confined as He is to symbols on a page, must
be consistent, a characteristic decidedly not tricksterish. As a result, in
modern Western culture the characteristics of tricksters are usually

considered to be shameful, disgraceful, naughty, bad, and certainly nothing that would ever create something good or admirable. Thus, it is hard for modern readers to understand how a trickster can be a thief and yet a culture hero, no matter what the Greeks say about Prometheus, who stole fire from the gods for the benefit of humankind. The more modern a Western trickster is, therefore, the more its tricksterish traits tend to be diluted. The tricksterism of fictional rather than mythological tricksters, such as Gandalf, must be presented as being engaged in for the forces of good in order to be acceptable; again, the hobbits, through whose eyes the events of the end of the Third Age are seen, always know that no matter how inexplicable, threatening, playful, heroic, or powerful Gandalf may appear to be, he is always to be trusted.

It is interesting that, despite the low esteem in which tricksterish traits are now held, fictional tricksters are rarely presented as being actually evil. (Even Loki has mitigating features.) They are, perhaps, too incompetent for the modern conception of evil, based as it is on notions of mechanistic efficiency, the banality of evil, the dogmatism of totalitarianism. Sauron, for instance, is not a trickster, deceiver though he may be. He is actually defeated because he does not have the flexibility of mind to anticipate the accidents of fate and personality that lead Frodo, Sam, and Gollum to Mount Doom. Saruman's seductive voice is a tricksterish trait (marked speech), but as his corruption is exposed, his ability to sway men's minds fades: He loses his capacity for magic. Likewise, in mythology, Loki becomes less tricksterish as his hatred for the gods of Asgard overwhelms him and his quest for vengeance becomes increasingly single-minded.

Tricksterism, it seems, is not compatible with concentration or with emotional investment: The best tricksters are flighty flibbertigibbets, and again, this is where Gandalf is only trickster-like, not completely tricky.

The universal popularity of the trickster figure in world mythology is an acknowledgment of the necessity for at least a minimal amount of chaos (a tolerated margin of mess). It is noticeable that the more authoritarian and humorless official culture is, the more vulnerable it is to the dangerous energy of trickster figures. Elvis Presley was a swing of the trickster pendulum to counterbalance the hysteria of Joseph McCarthy's congressional anti-Communist inquisitions.

Likewise, the hobbits of the Shire appear to have been vulnerable to the mere remnant of Saruman's tricky, persuasive voice because of their general bent toward conformity, cultural stasis, and distrust of anything different ("Tookish"). As a result, they found themselves virtually enslaved and the beauty of their homeland destroyed by Saruman's vile machines. It takes the energy of the returned heroes — who have learned the value of a little chaos under Gandalf's tutelage — to scour the Shire of this pollution and, since the past cannot be simply restored as though Sharkey never happened, to create a new order in his wake.

6. Fairies By Any Other Name

ELVES & THE TUATHA DÉ DANANN

The saddest consequence of the end of the Third Age is the loss of the Elves* — with their beauty, their wisdom, and their song. Elves were seminal to Tolkien's conception of Middle-earth from the very beginning; the core story of his entire Silmarillion mythology was the love between a mortal man and an Elvish woman, Beren and Lúthien, who he openly acknowledged symbolized the love affair between himself and his wife Edith.

The key image of this relationship was of the man watching the woman sing and dance in the woods, an idyllic vision removed from the horrors of war (from which both Tolkien, recovering from shell shock, and Beren, sole survivor of his people, were fleeing). The Elves are beings of starlight, immortal and ageless although subject to death by means of weapons or as a result of grief; men, in contrast, are beings of sunlight and are mortal.

* Note: I follow Tolkien's usage here when referring to the Elves of Middle-earth; he almost always capitalized the word Elves or Elvish, except in *The Hobbit*.

Although no race of Middle-earth is completely incapable of any of the arts, each has its specialty, and the arts of the Elves are music and poetry. Dwarves, in contrast, specialize in smithcrafts, the creation of beautiful objects and weapons, while hobbits seem to specialize in the culinary arts.

In *The Silmarillion*, Tolkien explains how the Elves were called to the Undying Lands of the West after the defeat of Melkor/Morgoth, although there were some who preferred to stay in Middle-earth. The Second Age is the age in which the Elves are the dominant race and the primary conflict during this age is between Elves and Sauron, Morgoth's lieutenant. This is the age in which Sauron insinuated himself into Elven graces and forges his rings of power; after his treachery is revealed, Númenórean men and Elves begin their alliance, culminating in the Battle of Dagorlad, in which Sauron is overthrown and the One Ring cut from his finger. The Third Age, which then ensues, is the age in which men, Elves, dwarves, hobbits, and even orcs are on more or less equal footing. Each race has its own sphere of influence and alliances between the races are minimal until the War of the Ring, when good and evil races must join their separate forces to battle for dominance.

The result of the final overthrow of Sauron and the destruction of his Ring, however, is that the remaining Elves of Middle-earth depart for the Undying Lands and men come to dominate, while the smaller races — the hobbits and dwarves — eventually dwindle into folklore. (Tolkien did conceive of his Middle-earth as the lost, archaic era of our own world, not as an alternate fantasy universe. Middle-earth's Fourth Age is, ultimately, the precursor of the modern world we all live in; some of his descriptions of the geological convulsions that formed Middle-earth suggest that he had heard of the plate tectonic theories being formulated at Oxford's department of earth science in the 1930's, such as the ideas of supercontinents that broke up into the current continental landmasses, and incorporated them into his Middle-earth cosmogony.)

The underlying societal structure of Middle-earth is that the Elves were there first, and then men came. After a period in which Elves and men coexisted, the immortal Elves slowly retreated to a land in the western sea, leaving Middle-earth to men. This parallels almost exactly the Irish legends of the Tuatha Dé Danann, the "fairy folk" who preceded the mortal Sons of Míl as the inhabitants of Ireland. The Túatha Dé Danann were magical beings who emerged from the mists of the North, and among their number were the Dagda (the Good God), also known as Éochaid Ollathair (the Horsey All-father); his son Oengus, or the Mac ind Óg (the Young Son), the love god; Dían Cecht, the god of medicine; Nuadu Argetlam (Nuadu of the Silver Hand, a prosthesis which replaced the hand he lost in battle), their king; Lugh Samildánach (Lugh Equally-skilled-in-all-crafts), their hero; Manannán mac Lir, the sea god; and many more.

After the arrival of the Milesians, whom the Irish considered their ancestral race, Ireland was divided between the Tuatha Dé Danann and the Milesians, with the men getting the "upper" portion and the Tuatha Dé the "lower," which seems to have meant a division between the surface of the earth and underground. As a result, the Tuatha Dé Danann were conceived as living within the Neolithic burial mounds that dot the Irish landscape and are known as *sídhe*; the Tuatha Dé Danann are thus also known as *sídh*-folk.

One of the most notable *sídhe* was the burial mound of Newgrange, or Brúg na Bóinne, in the Boyne valley, which was said to be the home of Oengus, the son of the Dagda and Boand, the goddess of the river Boyne. Newgrange is famous for its orientation so that the rising sun on the days surrounding the winter solstice shines directly down the passage into the interior chamber. It is believed to have originally lighted up a carved stone on the back of the chamber. Interestingly, the Irish believed that the Tuatha Dé Danann experienced the seasons inside their *sídhe* as the opposite of the seasons in the upper/outer world; thus, when it was the winter solstice in Ireland, it was the summer solstice inside the *sídh*; pictures taken from the interior of the sunlight creeping up the passage in Newgrange on the winter solstice show that the light seems golden and springlike while the frosty landscape of winter can be seen outside, a sight that makes it seem that the seasons are reversed in and out of the *sídh*.

Medieval Irish mythology contained more than one location for the Otherworld, where the Tuatha Dé Danann lived. One location, probably the earlier and/or original conception, was within the *sídhe*, "underground" in general. Another location was beneath a lake, under both earth and water. This is seen most strongly in the story of *The Pursuit of the Gilla Decair*, who is a surly servant who steals one of Finn mac Cumhail's horses and dives down into a lake; when Finn's champion Diarmuid follows, he finds himself in the Otherworld. The other location of the Otherworld is an island over the ocean to the west, a place sometimes called Hy Brasil, which is actually the origin of the name of the country Brazil in South America. The overseas Otherworld island is sometimes described as being ruled by the Tuatha Dé Danann god Manannán mac Lir, sometimes as being ruled by a beautiful woman.

Island Otherworlds sometimes are highly specialized. In the stories of *The Voyage of Bran*, *The Voyage of Snédgus and Mac Riagla*, *The Voyage of Maeldúin* and *The Voyage of Saint Brendan*, mariners encounter an island where everyone stands around laughing and gaping; an island where everyone wails and mourns; an island inhabited only by women; an island divided into black and white halves, where the wool of sheep who move from one side to the other changes color according to their location; an island that is completely uninhabited except for a small kitten jumping between pillars, who leaps straight through a mariner who tries to steal a necklace so that the man turns into a heap of ashes; an island of huge ants; an island of burning pigs; and so on. (Tolkien's friend C. S. Lewis utilized the tale type of the Irish Otherworldly voyage in his Narnia book, *The Voyage of the Dawn Treader*.)

The idea of the Grey Havens and the Undying Lands, which are the Elves' true home, is virtually identical to this idea of an overseas Otherworld inhabited by the Tuatha Dé Danann. Another common aspect of the Irish *sídh*-folk was that time spent with them in their Otherworld passed at a different speed than time in the mortal world; a person who spends a year with the Fair Folk may return to the mortal world to discover that a century has elapsed. Similarly, when the Fellowship spends a few days in Lothlórien, they are confused to find the moon's phases, as they think, out of joint when they emerge; it turns out that those "few days" were actually a month in the outside world.

The fact that Tolkien conceived of his Elves as equivalent to the Tuatha Dé Danann is literally illustrated in *The Hobbit*. His drawing of the Elvenking's Gate that accompanies Chapter 9, "Barrels Out of Bond," is a perfect illustration of a Newgrange-like mound with a passage burrowing into it. The Wood-Elves of this mound hold the dwarves prisoner and Bilbo, their burglar, must free them. This situation also has some parallels with the Middle English poem *Sir Orfeo*, which was one of the works that Tolkien taught in his seminars at Oxford; in that poem, Sir Orfeo's wife Heurodis is taken by the Fairy King and held within his castle, which sits in the midst of a wide green plain *within* a mountain. When Sir Orfeo follows the fairies into the mountain and castle, he sees the fairies' captives lying in the positions in which they were taken, some sleeping, others wounded, women in childbirth, madmen in bounds. Although the descriptions seem to depict people who should be dead (those who have been decapitated, for instance, usually do not live long), the poem says that they are people who are thought to be dead but actually are not.

This motif of people being held, undead, by the fairies is found in many Celtic folktales, usually of the "fairy midwife" type (a human midwife is brought by a fairy man to attend to his wife in her labor; she turns out to be a mortal woman everyone thought was dead). The tale type that Tolkien seems to be following here, however, is the one in which supernatural beings need the assistance of a mortal man to defeat a supernatural enemy, only in this case, it is the dwarves who need the assistance of a hobbit. The Elves of Lothlórien, for their part, live in what seems to be a sacred grove, which was characteristic of the religions of both the pagan Celts and the pagan Scandinavians.

The Wood-Elves that Bilbo and the dwarves encounter in *The Hobbit* are not quite as benevolent as the "high" Elves, such as Galadriel and Celeborn; Tolkien remarks that they are "more danger-ous and less wise." (H, p. 151) This distinction may be an echo of the Norse distinction between dark elves and light elves, although some scholars suspect that this distinction itself arose under the influence of Christianity. Nonetheless, the Wood-Elves are Elves and therefore "Good People." (H, p. 152) This is one of the euphemistic names for the fairies common in Ireland, *Daoine Maithe*; they are also known as the People of Peace, the Fair Family, the Gentle Folk, the Kind People, and most significantly, the Gentry. The Tuatha Dé Danann are of higher class, higher rank than the common folk (in contrast to the rather malevolent elves of Germanic tradition, who are in many ways indistinguishable from dwarves); likewise, the Elves are beyond all argument the aristocrats of Middle-earth, and those men who are most noble are not only described as having something Elvish about their demeanor but also often have Elvish blood somewhere in their ancestry and/or come from a race (such as the Númenóreans) that is anciently allied with Elves.

It is interesting that Tolkien chooses to call these beings "Elves," which are beings of a rather different sort in Old English tradition. It may be that he wanted to avoid the post-Victorian connotations of the term "fairy," which by the early twentieth century denoted tiny, delicate, winged creatures clad in gossamer who flitted amongst the flowers at the bottom of the garden. Fairies, by the time that Tolkien was writing *The Hobbit*, carried an aura of inescapable cuteness and an imperfect grasp of the facts of life, epitomized by P. G. Wodehouse's character, the insufferable dimwit Madeline Bassett, who believed that "Every time a fairy blows its wee nose, a baby is born." Tolkien's Fair Folk are much more powerful and noble creatures.

The Germanic elves at his disposal, however, while not quite as adorable as Victorian fairies, were not quite noble enough for his purposes. Their primary role in popular belief was as agents of disease, especially the more inexplicable and sudden illnesses. Even today, the term "stroke" for an arterial tear or blood clot in the brain comes from the notion that it is caused by a stroke from an elf's invisible arrow; a number of diseases of livestock, likewise, were explained as being the result of "elf-shot" well into the modern era. In fact, Stone Age flint arrowheads that work their way to the earth's surface, often as a result of plowing, were what was usually identified as the Elves' maleficent projectile. These arrowheads were obviously meant to be shot at someone or something, but they were not made by any people known to those who plowed them up. Elves were also sometimes suspected as the culprits when horses were found sweating and panting in the morning after being stabled all night; they were said to be elf-ridden, fairy-ridden, or hag-ridden, and thus elves were associated with witches and the *mara* or nightmare.

Other elves are called land-elves and appear to be spirits associated with specific places. In Iceland, the land-elves could be called upon to avenge injustice. These elves were often to be found in the vicinity of burial mounds, and the popularity of the element *Alf-* ("elf") in Old English names might indicate that these elves were conceived as some kind of ancestral fertility spirits whose benevolence could be bought, or at least flattered.

Germanic elves, therefore, were invisible or hard-to-see super-natural beings who inflicted disease on man and beast, and were therefore antagonistic to men. Even their association with the land opens the possibility of elf-human conflict if the land-elves are not properly appeased or they disapprove of human activity. In the pagan era, Germanic elves were thought to be related to the gods, the Esir, but on a slightly lower plane: demi-gods rather than full gods. In the Old Norse Eddas, the formulaic address to "Esir and the elves" is often found where "Esir and Vanir" might be expected, suggesting that on some level "elves" and "Vanir" (the primitive fertility gods who are displaced and then assimilated by the Esir) are equivalent; certainly the Elves' home Alfheim is said to belong to the Vanir god Freyr. Even if the Germanic elves are related to the Vanir, however, the Vanir were very definitely the "lower class" of the Norse gods. In any case, after the Germanic peoples became Christian, the originally amoral elves slowly came to be regarded as actively demonic beings.

The status of the Irish Tuatha Dé Danann also decreased in the post-Christian era but not to such a degree as the Germanic elves, perhaps because the Tuatha Dé were originally full gods. A popular Irish belief that lasted well into the nineteenth century held that when Lucifer rebelled against God, there were many angels who sided with him and fell into Hell along with him, but there were others who were committed to neither God nor Lucifer and as a result were shut out of Heaven but not accepted in Hell. These exiled — amoral — angels were said to be the Good People of Ireland. They could not be regarded as completely holy, because they had not sided with God, but neither were they completely evil, as actual demons and devils might be.

Tolkien's Elves of Middle-earth held this same ambivalent moral origin. When the cosmos emerged from the void, there were two orders of beings, the Ainur (gods, of whom Melkor was one) and the Maiar (demi-gods, of whom Gandalf was one). The cosmos was created through song, and Melkor corrupted this song through introducing a literal discord within it. Those Maiar and Valar who joined Melkor's chorus parallel the angels who fell with Lucifer.

According to Tolkien, the ages of the cosmos were the Ages of the Lamps, the Ages of the Trees, the Ages of Darkness, the Ages of the Stars, and finally the Ages of the Sun. The Elves awakened during the first Age of the Stars, while men awakened during the first Age of the Sun. When Melkor stole the Silmarils from Fëanor, the Noldor Elves swore vengeance and, in their single-minded quest to recover their treasures, committed crimes against other Elves along the way. Of all the Noldor, only Galadriel survived the War of the Silmarils, and she wore one of the Elven Rings forged in conjunction with Sauron. These Elves, although not evil, are nonetheless tainted by their bent for vengeance; their association with Sauron, however well- meaning it was at the time; and their attachment to Middle-earth. They are not quite as pure as the Elves who withdrew from Middle-earth for the Undying Lands. In this way, the Elves of Middle-earth parallel the Tuatha Dé Danann, who fell from Heaven but did not make it all the way to Hell.

As with Gandalf, whom the hobbits know to be on the side of good although the men of Rohan and Gondor have suspicions about his true allegiances, Galadriel the Elf-Queen is viewed with suspicion by Boromir and, initially, Gimli. Whereas Galadriel's soul-searching of the members of the Fellowship was harmless to those with pure hearts, Boromir's ambivalence regarding the Ring surfaces under her scrutiny and he projects his own duplicity onto her. Gimli, however, who is suspicious of Elves as an automatic cultural reflex, immediately falls under Galadriel's spell, his heart won by her empathy for dwarvish homesickness for Khazad-dûm, her own sense of exile from the Undying Lands echoing the dwarves' sense of exile from their home-land.

The Elf-Queen is an ambivalent character in British folklore. Her most famous appearance is probably in the Scottish ballad and legend of Thomas the Rhymer. The thirteenth century figure Thomas Learmont, the laird of Erceldoune, is said to have been taken into Fairyland or Elfland by the Elf-Queen for seven years, which pass as though hardly the space of a day (like the passage of time in the *sídh* and in Lothlórien). The Elf-Queen shows Thomas three paths: one, the hard, thorn-covered path, is the little-traveled path of righteousness; the broad, easy path is the path of wickedness, although some think that it is the road to Heaven; and the middle path, winding over the hills, is the path to Elfland. Elfland, therefore, is neither Heaven nor Hell, but a different place altogether. (However, the rivers that bound Elfland run with blood, all the blood shed in the mortal world.)

In Elfland, the Elf-Queen gives Thomas a coat and a pair of shoes, but most importantly she gives him an apple that bestows poetic skill upon him, and thus when he returns to the mortal world he becomes known as the Rhymer, renowned as a prophet. The Elf-Queen is an ambivalent character — she bestows the gift of prophecy, but at great risk (if Thomas spoke a single word in Elfland he would never have been able to return, much like Persephone being trapped in Hades if she ate anything there), the journey on which she takes Thomas loses him seven years, and prophecy, as the Trojan princess Cassandra learned, is a dubious gift. Knowing the future does not necessarily allow one to change it.

The gifts that the Elf-Queen bestows on Thomas the Rhymer have the same ambivalence as the visions that Galadriel shows Sam and Frodo in her mirror. What the hobbits see is true, but they have no way of stopping what they see from occurring, and also, the meaning of what they see is not necessarily what they assume it to be. Sam sees Frodo apparently lying dead; he does not realize that not only is Frodo not dead, only poisoned by Shelob, but that the reason he is lying all alone in the dark is because Sam will abandon his body in

Cirith Ungol under the influence of the Ring. The devastation of the Shire that Sam sees is the result of the hobbits' "mercy" in not killing Saruman when there was the chance. Prophecy, as we will discuss in the context of riddles, is a tricky thing.

When the Elves leave Middle-earth, they take magic with them. Even though dwarves, hobbits, and Ents remain, it is men who will dominate from now on. Magic will be displaced by science and technology. Melkor and Sauron may have been defeated, but the price to be paid for that defeat was high. Tolkien seems to imply that the price may indeed have been too high: Magic may be gone, but it is still yearned for and technology has stepped in to fill that gap. The pollution and destruction of the natural world that Saruman inflicted on Isengard remains while the songs of the Elves are gone. It is only through telling stories that the memory of the Elves remains.

7. Crafty & Deep

DWARVES

For all the Celtic influences that the Anglo-Saxonist Tolkien slipped under the radar in writing his fiction, his dwarves are completely and unmistakably Germanic. (As with his insistence on the form "Elves" rather than "elfs," Tolkien insisted on the form "dwarves" rather than "dwarfs," in part to emphasize their ancientness and in part to distinguish them from quaint Victorian notions of dwarves.) Their very names come from the *Voluspá* section of the Elder Edda, a list known as the *Dvergatal* or, appropriately enough, the "List of Dwarves." The same list appears in Snorri Sturluson's Prose Edda. The dwarves, says Snorri, originally arose from the giant Ymir's flesh (which became earth when the giant was killed) as maggots in rotting flesh, but then the gods decided to give them the shape of and intelligence of men, but on a smaller scale. Unlike men, they lived in (under) the earth and in rocks.

There are a number of familiar names in the Edda's List of Dwarves, with some slight spelling modifications: Thorin (Oakenshield), Kíli, Fíli, Dwalin, Óin, Glóin, Dori, Ori, Nori, Bifur, Bofur, and Bombur, not to mention Gandalf himself. Only Balin is missing; his name fits into the rhyming schemes that Tolkien has established for his band, but the name Balin itself actually comes from the *Suite du Merlin* and Thomas Malory's *Morte d'Arthur*, where he is a knight paired with his identical twin brother Balan, and the name probably derives ultimately from the Celtic sun-god Beli. Tolkien's dwarves, like Norse mythology's dwarves, are master metallurgists: miners, smiths, and jewelers. They live under and inside the earth, close to the metal ores and gems they work with. They are short of stature, thickset, and bearded; their weapon of choice is the axe. The dwarves of Norse mythology are preservers of lore and of poetry; Tolkien describes his dwarves also as having long memories, especially for insults. They live by a stringent code of honor, but their weakness is their greed. They do not like to share; they do not play well with others.

There is something about the dwarves of myth that suggests that they are, ultimately, somehow associated with death and the dead. Partly this is because of their dwelling within the earth — the place where humans go only when they are buried (or miners). The association is made stronger by the fact that the peoples of Iron Age Northern Europe buried important people with rich grave goods, the kinds of things that dwarves might make, and raised burial mounds with the inhumation placed in a chamber inside the mound, the kind of place where dwarves (or fairies) might live. The greediness of dwarves might thus be connected with the widespread notion that the dead are greedy, greedy for life, for all the things that they have left behind. (This is why ghosts, vampires, and other revenants are a danger to the living, and why ancestors must be appeased.) The curses that dwarves place on treasures stolen or tricked from them are similar to the curses believed to follow stolen grave goods: no matter how beautiful or desirable the object, owning it will bring only bad luck until it is returned to its proper owner.

The dwarves' creativity, however, also echoes the flip side of death: life. Short, earthy figures in mythology are often associated with fertility (as the dead decay into the earth around them and become part of the creation of new life). Celtic goddesses such as the Matrones (the Mothers) were often depicted accompanied by short, stocky, hooded figures called *genii cucullati*, "hooded spirits," who carried eggs, moneybags, or other symbols of fertility. Sometimes the *genius cucllatus* served as a kind of lampshade, and when the hooded cloak was removed, the lamp itself was seen to be the figure's phallus. The phallic symbolism of short, chthonic beings is found in many mythologies throughout the world. Some scholars have suggested that Germanic dwarves were considered to be the midwives to the metal ores within the earth; the ores, for their part, were perceived as being embryos forming and maturing within the womb of the earth.

The discovery of how to work metal was a crucial development in human history. Although organized human societies began to form in the Stone Ages, the use of metals — copper, bronze, and most importantly iron — required serious reorganization of human life. Since metal ores are found only at specific places on the planet, as opposed to rocks, which are everywhere, trade routes became necessary to transport the raw materials or the worked items themselves. Complete self-sufficiency was no longer practical. During the Bronze Age, when the dominant metal was an alloy of tin and copper, two metals not necessarily found in close proximity to each other, trade was often vitally necessary in order to make bronze at all. It was possible for a people located near veins of metal to become significantly wealthier than the people who lived in metal-poor areas, and for people who traveled between the two to become richest of all. These long-distance traders transmitted not only goods from place to place, but also languages and technologies.

Archaeologist Barry Cunliffe, for example, suggests that the spread of the Celtic languages, with associated material culture, throughout Iron Age Europe was as a result of the trade in iron goods — if you wanted to buy the stuff and wanted to learn how to make it yourself, you needed to be able to communicate with those who already had that knowledge. This may also have been the reason for the spread of the Indo-European languages in general.

The Bronze Age in Europe began between 2400 and 1600 B.C. and was replaced by the Iron Age roughly 1000-800 B.C., depending on location. In Northern Europe, the Iron Age is associated with the Celtic and Germanic cultures, and basically lasted up to the point of Christianization. Christianity, for its part, was the medium by which literacy reached these peoples, and thus the "pagan" mythological material written down for the first time in the early Middle Ages in Northern Europe generally reflects the concerns of the immediately preceding Iron Age society. Within these myths, the figure of the smith is a magical, often rather threatening one.

Wayland was the smith-god of Germanic myth, taught by trolls and lame in one leg. His lameness associates him with the Greek smith-god Hephaistos and his Roman cognate Vulcan. Lameness or "one-footedness" is often associated with the ability to travel between the worlds of the living and the dead (with one "live" foot and one "dead" foot), according to the historian Carlo Ginzburg in his 1991 study *Ecstasies: Deciphering the Witches' Sabbath*. Ginzburg, following Mircea Eliade's work on shamanism, sees stories in which an animal is killed and eaten, then resurrected through its skin and bones, as an echo of shamanic initiation; in the story, the shaman warns the diners that they must not break the bones for the marrow, and one of them invariably does, with the result that the resurrected animal is lame (one foot is alive, the other retains the mark of what happened to it when it was dead). In Germanic culture, this story is told about Thor and the two goats, Tanngnost and Tanngrisi, that draw his chariot, and the diners who crack the goat's bones are giants. Thor, therefore, is a "dwarf" in comparison to them, and incidentally, his trademark weapon is a dwarf-made hammer, symbolically interchangeable with the axe. (The smith hammers metal into a blade; both are weapons used for striking; the shape of the hammer and the axe are difficult to distinguish iconographically.)

Smith-gods such as Wayland and Hephaistos make magical armor for warriors. The shield that Hephaistos creates for Achilles is a crucial implement in the Trojan War, and it is probably not coincidence that Achilles himself, while not literally lame, has one impervious foot and, on the other, his fabled "Achilles' heel," which is the one place where death can enter Achilles' body. There are references in *Beowulf* to the hero's chain mail coat having been made by Wayland, and the sword Mimming in the Old English poem *Waldere* is also of his making. In the poem *Völundarkvida* in the Poetic Edda, the story is told of how King Nídudr lamed Wayland and forced him to work in his royal smithy, and in retaliation the smith killed the king's two sons and made drinking cups out of their skulls, raped the king's daughter, and flew away through the air. Wayland thus, although not a dwarf (indeed the *Völundarkvida* calls him "the prince of elves," although there is a certain overlap between "dark elves" and dwarves in the Eddas), shows the same characteristics of craftsmanship and revenge associated with those beings.

These traits are seen in many of the tales told about dwarves and their works. For instance, the dwarves made all of the magical equipment associated with the Esir and Vanir deities. According to the *Skáldskaparmál*, Loki sneakily cut off Thor's wife Sif's beautiful yellow hair, and in order to placate the enraged god, he promised to get dwarves to make real golden hair to replace it. The dwarves he recruited made not only the hair, but the magic ship Skidbladnir for Freyr (it could sail against both wind and tide) and the magic spear Gungnir for Odin. Loki then bet his head to another set of dwarves that they could not beat that achievement, and they made the gold boar Gullinbursti for Freyr, Thor's unbeatable hammer Mjollnir, and the gold armring Draupnir, which dropped eight more gold rings every ninth night. Loki lost his bet, but managed to avoid paying his head by pointing out that the bet covered his head but not his neck. The dwarves got their revenge by sewing up Loki's lips instead.

Another time Loki tricked the shape-shifting dwarf Andvari out of his stock of gold by catching him when he was in the shape of a pike. When he had got all the raw gold, he saw that the dwarf was keeping back one, cunningly wrought ring that he was holding in his hand. Loki demanded that ring, too; Andvari turned it over, but attached a curse to it and all the gold that Loki took from him, that it would only bring tragedy and woe to whoever possessed it. Loki used the curse to his advantage, however, by using the gold and the ring to pay the weregild (a fine for having killed someone, payable to the dead man's family by the murderer's family) for a man named Otter whom he had killed, passing the curse to Otter's family. He nearly passed the cursed ring on to Odin first, however, and this bit of potential treachery was one of the gods' first intimations of just how little they could trust the trickster.

In Germanic mythology, dwarves tend to be relatively solitary creatures or to come in small sets of three or four. The notion of a band as large as Thorin's expedition of thirteen (thereby requiring an additional burglar to make the numbers lucky) is unusual. However, the traditional dwarves, like Tolkien's, are a predominantly male race. Indeed, some myths suggest that they do not reproduce sexually at all — hence the comparison of their creation from Ymir's flesh as being "like maggots." In the ancient and medieval world, maggots were believed to spontaneously, asexually generate from dead flesh, since their eggs were invisible to the human eye. At the same time, mythological dwarves were not immune to sexual desire: The only way Freya could acquire her dwarf-wrought necklace Brisingamen was by sleeping with each of the four dwarves who made it, and this is regarded by the other gods as incredibly demeaning.

The etymology of the word "dwarf" is unclear. The main contenders for the word's root are Indo-European *dhuer-, "damage," Old

Indian *dhvaras*, "demonic being," and Indo-European **dreugh*, "dream," but also the root of German *Trug*, "deception." The most interesting of these possibilities is **dhuer-*. In contrast to elves, who are depicted as being beautiful and "other," dwarves are depicted as being of human form but misshapen. Their outstanding characteristic is not their size but their deformity, and the fact of the matter is, until the late twentieth century, people generally believed that a beautiful appearance indicated both a beautiful soul and an admirable moral character, while physical ugliness indicated metaphysical monstrosity as well. The irony and the paradox of dwarves, then, was that such ugly beings could create works of such beauty. In some ways, they represented the uglinesses of human character: greed, lust, vindictiveness, obsession. The objects they made could arouse all these emotions.

At the same time, dwarves had a connection with wisdom and knowledge (not always the same thing). The Norse myth of how Odin acquired the mead of poetry shows poetic wisdom created first by all the gods spitting into a cauldron; the spittle was formed into a man named Kvasir who epitomized the combined wisdom of all the gods. Two dwarves named Fjalar and Galar conspired to murder Kvasir, drain him of his blood, and mix the blood with honey and water to brew a mead that contained all Kvasir's wisdom. Eventually the dwarves had to use the mead to pay weregild to a giant named Suttung after they murdered his parents. Suttung set his daughter Gunnlod to guard the mead, but Odin disguised himself and tricked Gunnlod into sleeping with him and then allowing him three drinks of the mead. He swallowed it all in three quaffs, shape-shifted to an eagle, and flew back with bulging cheeks to Asgard, where he spat nearly all the mead out into every container that the gods could muster. However, along the way, he had spilled some of the mead over Midgard, and that is the mead of poetry available to human poets. Poetic wisdom thus cycles from the gods, to humans, to dwarves, to giants, and then back to the gods again, with a little dealt out to humans in the process.

The dwarf Regin was the foster-father of the hero Sigurd. He trained and helped the hero to slay the dragon Fáfnir, who guarded a marvelous hoard of gold — it was, in fact, the gold that Loki had tricked away from Andvari to use as Otter's weregild. Fáfnir and Regin were the brothers of Otter, and under the influence of the cursed gold, the two brothers killed their father to get their hands on it, but then fell out over the division of the spoils. Originally human, Fáfnir turned into a dragon to guard the gold, while Regin turned into a dwarf ("deformed" by his jealousy and hatred of his brother, perhaps). Regin had to re-forge Sigurd's father's broken sword in order to get him a weapon strong enough to withstand the combat ahead of the hero. He told Sigurd to dig a trench along the trail from Fáfnir's lair to his watering hole and stab his soft underbelly as he passed over the trench. When Sigurd drank the blood of the dragon and ate its roasted heart, he gained the ability to understand the language of birds, and he realized that Regin intended to kill him to get the gold for himself. Sigurd therefore decapitated his treacherous foster-father and took the gold himself.

This story has resonances throughout both *The Hobbit* and *The Lord of the Rings* — Smaug's soft underbelly, the language of birds, the greedy madness caused by hoards of gold, the hero's reforged sword. (Enlightenment through drinking a magic liquid meant for another also resonates with the story of Gwion Bach's transformation into Taliesin.)

In the *Nibelungenlied*, the dwarf king Alberich is a pivotal character, although he does not occur elsewhere in Germanic mythology. He is the dwarf who stole the Rhinegold from the Rhine maidens and forged a ring out of it. He lived in a subterranean castle carved out of rock and ornamented with gems (echoed in Khazad-dûm). Tolkien was notoriously short-tempered at any suggestion that his Ring cycle was influenced by Richard Wagner's operatic Ring Cycle based on the Nibelung saga. The fact was, Tolkien and Wagner were independently influenced by the same myth, and Tolkien considered that Wagner told the story wrong, just as he felt Shakespeare got the Birnam Wood story wrong (see Chapter 4).

In later medieval literature, dwarves often occur as the sidekicks of knights. In Arthurian romances, the knight's dwarf is a companion, a servant, and especially a messenger. Lotte Motz, in *The Wise One of the Mountains*, points out that dwarves in mythology are, in essence, servants of the gods; this role continues in the medieval literature, where they are servants of the aristocracy. The mythological dwarves were helpful to gods and humans, but always in accordance with their own, usually vengeful, agendas. Literary dwarves tended to be simply helpful, subordinate to their larger employers.

Tolkein's dwarves manifest some of the negative characteristics of mythological dwarves, but these are shown as being weaknesses to which they succumb — especially the gold-lust that falls upon Thorin and his band when they reach the Lonely Mountain — rather than defining elements of their personalities. Balin's desire to re-establish Khazad-dûm is presented as a perhaps dangerous but nonetheless noble attempt to recapture the grandeur and artistic excellence of an earlier age; the rousing of the Balrog may be a warning against dwarvish hubris, but the Balrog is an evil external to the dwarves, a thing to which they fall prey rather than an emanation of some inner evil. In fact, when Glóin remarks that part of Balin's mission in returning to Moria was to try to find one of the last known dwarvish rings, the ring of Thrór, there is a hint that the dwarves have been lured by the stirring of Sauron's evil against their knowledge or will.

Gimli, Glóin's son, is the character who moves Tolkien's dwarves out of the dubious moral realm of the mythological dwarf and into the more noble realm of romance. For the first leg of the Fellowship's journey, he is simply one among many, prone to cryptic, dark, poetic statements. He is contrasted from the start with the light, ethereal elf Legolas, and their interspecies sparring begins as authentic antagonism. After the disaster on the bridge in Moria, when Gandalf plunges into the abyss, Gimli appears to reach a personal turning point. Up to this time, his goal had been reunion with his own people; discovering the colony in Moria to be destroyed, his old allegiance is no longer operative, and in Lothlórien, he sees Galadriel and pledges his loyalty to her. From this point, the competition between Elf and Dwarf becomes friendly, with each trying to persuade the other of the beauty of his way of life. Their goal is no longer mutual denigration but mutual enlightenment.

After the breaking of the Fellowship, Gimli and Legolas become Aragorn's constant companions, and this is when Gimli makes the transition from mythic to romance dwarf. He is the hero's sidekick, the loyal companion who trembles to traverse the Paths of the Dead but whose loyalty to his king outweighs his fear.

Throughout his novels, Tolkien makes a habit of narrating scenes from the "lowest" point of view. His protagonists are always "little guys," quite literally. For the most part, his "little guys" are hobbits, but when there are no hobbits available, Gimli has the proper stature for Tolkien's preferred point of view. When Aragorn, Legolas, and Gimli encounter the Rohirrim, for instance, as they ride off on their borrowed horses, it is Gimli who is described as looking back from his precarious seat behind Legolas to see the men of Rohan disappearing in the distance. He is the one who shivers in the cold and then makes a fire to warm them; he is the one who looks up to see the enigmatic wanderer, Gandalf, gazing at them from the clearing's edge. He is the one who breaks the polite exchange of words from Treebeard's messengers — Merry and Pippin — to Théoden's army arriving at Isengard, turning diplomacy into a reunion of comrades-at-arms. He attends the meeting between Saruman and Gandalf with the intention of gauging whether the two wizards really look alike, and so the scene is constantly subtitled, as it were, with Gimli's comments, and it is he who first breaks free of the spell of Saruman's voice: "The words of this wizard stand on their heads. . . . In the language of Orthanc help means ruin, and saving means slaying, that is plain." (TT, p. 184)

In Gimli, the dwarf's earthiness becomes plain common sense. Greed is redeemed by devotion to the true king.

8. The Land Beneath the Waves

Númenor, Atlantis, Lyonesse, Ys & the Cantre'r Gwaelod

In the same letter in which Tolkien told W. H. Auden about his distaste for Shakespeare's treatment of Birnam Wood, he mentioned that he had a recurring dream about "the Great Wave, towering up, and coming in ineluctably over the trees and green fields" (*Letters*, p. 213) and that this was both the source of his vision of the downfall of Númenor and that it ended when he had finally written down the story.

Tolkien seems to have viewed this dream as something heritable; he says that his parents died when he was too young to have known whether they had the dream, but he discovered, after *The Lord of the Rings* was published with Tolkien's own dream attributed to Faramir, that his son Michael also dreamed it. Tolkien appears to have regarded this as a personal dream and evidence of familial, even tribal inheritance, although those schooled in the psychoanalytical theory of dream interpretation might be more likely to see it as a fairly common dream image of being "overwhelmed" by repressed emotion, depicted through a dream's typically literal and concrete imagery.

Writing down the dream released the power of the image over Tolkien's unconscious by bringing it up to the conscious level of his mind. In any case, the dream gave Tolkien a sense of being connected to some much larger dimension of human history, a connection to what Carl Jung would call the collective unconscious (although Tolkien himself certainly would not).

Atlantis is only the most famous of the legends of sunken lands. Celtic mythology is particularly rife with them: There is the Cantre'r Gwaelod, the "Sunken Hundred" ("cantre/cantref" literally means "hundred households" and was an administrative unit something like a county) in Cardigan Bay off the coast near Borth in Wales; Lyonesse, the inundated land off the coast of Land's End in Cornwall, which was the homeland of the Arthurian hero Tristan; and the land of Ys off the coast of Brittany in the Bay of Douarnenez. There are certain similarities between all of these stories, many of which have echoes in Tolkien's story of Númenor.

The Atlantis story originates in Plato's dialogues *Timaeus* and *Critias*. In the *Critias*, the title character tells a story that he says has been passed down in his family from the time of Solon, who had heard the story from priests in Egypt. He says that some nine thousand years before, there was an island located beyond the straits of Gibralter on which was a marvelous city and civilization founded by Poseidon, the god of the sea. (Poseidon, it should be noted, had originally competed with Athena to be the patron deity of Plato's native city of Athens, so one might wonder whether this story is being told about a kind of shadow-Athens, a kind of "their-but-for-the-grace-of-Athena" story.)

The city, which Plato describes in detail, was perfectly and geometrically organized, technologically advanced, and its citizens were models of wisdom, piety, and virtue. Eventually, however, the Atlanteans became greedy and corrupt, and in retaliation the gods destroyed the city in an earthquake and tidal wave that together caused the island to sink beneath the waves forever. In the *Timaeus* Plato offers some additional information: The Atlantean empire stretched as far east as Egypt and through Europe to Tyrrhenia, the island was the size of Libya (North Africa) and Asia put together, that the island disappeared in the course of a single day and night, and that the sea is now impassable in that spot because of the underwater ruins. In this version, the downfall of Atlantis comes at the end of a war between Atlantis and Athens in which the Athenians got the upper hand, saving the Hellenes as a whole from slavery under Atlantis.

The ocean of ink that has been spent speculating about Atlantis is enough to drown the island all over again. It has been located in the Sargasso Sea, the Caribbean, the Andes, the Azores, the Antarctic, the Mediterranean islands of Santorini or Crete, western Turkey, even off the coast of Cornwall, conflating the stories of Atlantis and Lyonesse. The question of its location is intricately tied to the question of its age: There was no civilization sufficiently advanced twelve thousand years ago to correspond literally to the technological achievements attributed to the Atlanteans — not to mention that there was no Athens to best them in war at that time — so Plato must have been in error saying that the civilization existed nine thousand years before his time. If he was in error here, perhaps he was also in error placing the island out in the Atlantic Ocean.

The most generally accepted archaeological theory for the location of Atlantis holds that Plato, living in the fourth century B.C., was influenced in his story of Atlantis by oral traditions about the volcanic explosion of the island of Thera, now called Santorini, around 1500 B.C. This island is located north of Crete in the Aegean Sea and had a culture closely linked to Minoan Crete; it is believed that Thera's catastrophic eruption, which blew off the top of the island and caused half of it to sink into the sea, also caused climatic changes that contributed to the decay of Minoan civilization. The Minoans were technologically advanced, ruled an expansive large empire, traded with Egypt, and were the cultural predecessors of the Hellenic Greek civilization in which Plato lived (the later Minoan culture kept its records in an alphabet known as Linear B, which has been translated to reveal the language of Mycenaean Greece).

Tolkien began writing his story of the fall of Númenor in his unfinished story "The Lost Road," which he began writing in 1936. In *The Unfinished Tales* there is a description of Númenor: a five-sided island in the shape of a pentangle; the center section is 250 miles across, and each of the points is a separate region named for its geographic direction. Atlantis, according to the *Critias*, comprised five concentric rings of land, divided by canals, surrounding a central island; Plato gives the precise widths of each land-ring and canal and the central island. At the central point of Númenor is a mountain called Meneltarma, "the Pillar of the Heavens," dedicated to the worship of Middle-earth's high god Eru Ilúvatar; the center of Atlantis is a temple dedicated to the god Poseidon and his consort Cleito, who are not only the patron deities of the island but also the progenitors of its populace. The Númenoreans are, until the coming of Sauron, noble, peaceful, and pure; the Atlanteans were originally virtuous, law-abiding, sober, and ascetic. The parallels continue along the same lines.

The Valar had made Númenor for the men — the Edain — who had fought Morgoth with the Elves. Númenor was within sight, from the top of Meneltarma, of the Undying Lands of the Elves, but the Edain were forbidden to sail to the west to those lands or to ever set foot on them. Númenor was as far west as the race of men could travel. The Edain, while long-lived, were not immortal as the Elves were, and this proved the initial source of their envy of the Elves, by which Sauron, the overthrown Morgoth's deputy, gained a foothold in their hearts and minds.

Furthermore, as the Númenoreans expanded the range of their marine exploration, the more tempting the lands to the west became — much as the Atlanteans began to expand their empire throughout the Mediterranean. The Númenorean king Ar-Pharazôn determined to challenge Sauron for dominion of Middle-earth, but Sauron played humble and became the king's counselor instead, convincing him that if he were to conquer the Undying Lands, instead of Middle-earth, he would gain everlasting life — an echo of the Serpent's temptation of Eve. When Ar-Pharazôn set foot on the Undying Lands, the entire world changed in a cataclysm like that which overthrew Atlantis in a single day and night. Not only was Númenor overwhelmed by a towering wave — the green wave that haunts Faramir in his dreams, bringing everlasting darkness, as he tells Éowyn — but the Undying Lands were literally removed from the face of the earth. As Tolkien perceived it, the Undying Lands originally existed on the face of the globe, reached by normal sailing; after the cataclysm, the "lost road" that led to them left the curve of the globe on a tangent, placing the Undying Lands in some kind of other, outer space, unreachable by mortals.

The story of Atlantis has been the subject of so much speculation that it is often overlooked that stories of inundated lands are not unique to Plato and the Greeks. They are also common along the western coasts of Wales, Cornwall, and Brittany. The Welsh story of Cantre'r Gwaelod takes place roughly during the time of King Arthur. The king of the area was Gwyddno Garanhir (his first name means "famous for knowledge" and his epithet means something like "long shanks"; is it a coincidence that this epithet is also given to Aragorn — Strider — by the men of Bree?) who is, incidentally, the father of Elphin, a major character in the second half of the story of Taliesin. Gwyddno was said to own a marvelous food-basket that, when food for one man was put into it, would turn that portion into food for a hundred men. Gwyddno's land was beautiful and fertile, holding sixteen cities, but it lay below sea level and the waters were held back by a series of walls and drainage systems.

The man in charge of upkeep for the walls was Seithennin, son of Seithyn Saidi; one night Seithennin got drunk and let the sluices open, flooding the entire cantref. In some versions of the story, the only people to escape from the flood were Gwyn ap Llywarch and the king's daughter, galloping madly on a horse with the rising waters lapping at its hoofs. In other versions, including a poem found in the mid-thirteenth century *Black Book of Carmarthen* (one of the oldest surviving Welsh manuscripts, which also contains several poems attributed to Myrddin), the flood was caused not by Seithennin's drunken carelessness but by a woman named Mererid who left off the lid of a sacred well after a feast of some sort. The poem makes repeated, elliptical references to this carelessness being an act of pride: "After pride comes a long death. . . . After pride comes grief. . . . After pride comes offence. . . . After pride comes a distant death." It is said that the bells of the churches in the sixteen sunken cities can still be heard chiming under the sea when the winds are calm.

Of all the sunken lands, the Cantre'r Gwaelod has left the most visible remains; at extremely low tides, the remains of cultivated and inhabited lands can be seen out in Wales' Cardigan Bay off the coast of Borth, just north of Aberystwyth. There are also the remains of causeways running out into the bay that are said to be roads that served the cantref. It seems certain that the sea level was at one time much lower than it is now, and that inhabited lands were swallowed when the sea level rose, much as we are constantly warned will happen to modern coastal cities with the melting of the polar ice caps. There may also be a memory of this rising sea level preserved in the story of Branwen, the Second Branch of the Mabinogi, in which it is said that at the time of the story, the sea between Wales and Ireland was much smaller, and so Bran the Blessed (a giant) was able to wade across it to rescue his abused sister.

Cantre'r Gwaelod, then, was like Númenor in being a "constructed" land; the Welsh had reclaimed it from the sea (and to the sea it returned), while Númenor had been created by the Elves to reward the Edain for their support in the war against Morgoth. Like the Atlanteans and the Númenoreans, Cantre'r Gwaelod was a land of magical plenty that was lost as the result of human complacency, taking for granted the benefits that they enjoyed and failing to keep up the vigilance and moral rectitude needed to preserve them.

Lyonesse was said to lie between England's Land's End and the Scilly Isles. In fact, in 387 A.D. the would-be Roman emperor Maximus exiled a heretic to the Scilly Island, singular, suggesting that as late as then, the sea level was low enough that the mass of land that now pokes above the waves as several islands constituted a single land mass. Archaeological finds show that Mount's Bay was above water and inhabited at least into the second millennium B.C. Lyonesse held several towns and 140 churches, whose bells, like those of the Cantre'r Gwaelod, still chime beneath the waves when the weather is still.

The stories about the sinking of Lyonesse offer less consensus about the time and circumstances than some other sunken land tales. One version says that after Mordred's final battle with Arthur at Camlann, he chased the remnants of Arthur's army west into Lyonesse, where the ghost of Merlin appeared and caused the land to sink beneath him in revenge for his betrayal of the king, while Arthur's army made it to high ground on the newly formed Scilly Isles. Another story dates the sinking of the land very specifically to a huge storm on November 11, 1099. One man, named Trevilian, managed to escape the inundation on horseback, with the water lapping at his horse's heels. As a result, the Trevelyan family crest still shows a horse emerging from the waters. The most well-known inhabitant of Lyonesse was Tristan, the tragic lover of Iseult, and in some versions of his story, the reason he was living in his uncle King Mark's court in

Cornwall, where he became embroiled in this love affair, was because his inheritance had sunk beneath the waves, leaving him landless.

There are many parallels between Tristan and Aragorn, the heir of the kings of sunken Númenor, that we will explore in greater depth in the next chapter. The story that Lyonesse was inundated to punish Mordred for his rebellion against King Arthur is echoed in Tolkien's tale that Númenor was drowned to punish its inhabitants for rebelling against the strictures laid on them by the Valar.

The Breton legend of the city of Ys, or Ker-Is, blames the deluge of the city on the sinfulness of its princess, Dahut (also sometimes called Ahes). Dahut was the pagan daughter of King Gradlon, who converted to Christianity. Gradlon built Ys to please his daughter, and he kept the key to the dykes that held back the sea on a chain around his neck at all times. Dahut turned Ys into a city of debauchery, leading the way in all manner of sin. According to some, she took a new lover each night and suffocated him as the sun rose, dumping his body in the sea.

One day a stranger arrived in Ys and it was Dahut who was seduced for a change. He persuaded her to steal the dyke key from her father, at which a huge wave overwhelmed the city. Gradlon escaped on his horse Morvarc'h (which means "sea horse"), with Dahut clinging onto the horse's rear hoof as the waters rose, lapping at the horse's heels. The burden was too great for the horse, and as it slowed down, a vision of St. Gwenole (the saint responsible for Gradlon's conversion) appeared and commanded Gradlon to drop the princess. The father shoved his daughter back into the sea into which she had dumped so many lovers and escaped to higher ground. Dahut is said to have become a mermaid, still swimming through her old haunts in the sunken city of Ys, whose church bells, silenced during her pagan revelry, still chime beneath the waves. Here again is the motif of the few, morally superior survivors who escape the flood and the idea that the land is drowned because of pride and rebellion, which also underlies the story of Númenor. The devil who proves to be Dahut's downfall is paralleled in Sauron's seduction of the Númenoreans into breaking the Valars' commandment not to sail west from the island.

All of these stories suggest, to a greater or lesser extent, that these places were inundated because of some kind of sin, whether of pride, lust, drunkenness, or treachery. To this extent they echo the biblical story of Noah, in which God floods the earth because of the overall sinfulness of humankind. As with Noah, there is usually a single family unit that survives the inundation and to some extent repopulates what remains of the land. The motif of the few survivors of the cataclysm who escape to start anew in a less bountiful land is repeated throughout these stories, from Cantre'r Gwaelod to Lyonesse to Ys to Númenor. Interestingly, while this element is missing in the Atlantis myth as Plato tells it, one of the most fruitful areas of speculation in latter-day explications of the myth traces one or another of the great civilizations of the past to Atlantean refugees. Initially, Atlantis was claimed to be the source of the pyramid-builders of Egypt because, of course, primitive North Africans could hardly have come up with such advanced technology by themselves. By the same line of reasoning, the pyramids of South America must have been built by Atlanteans fleeing in the opposite direction. The myth of Atlantis has therefore been used to rationalize racist assumptions about the capacities of non-European peoples.

The Celtic tales have a bias toward blaming the flood on a woman, who acts deliberately or innocently. These stories seem to have some connection with Irish tales in which a woman recklessly takes the lid off of a well that overflows, becoming the source of a river such as the Boyne or Shannon. This, in turn, suggests that these legendary women are the descendants of Celtic water goddesses of various sorts. Some interpretations of the legend of Ys suggest that Dahut's "debauchery" is an indication that she was practicing pagan rites in an era when Brittany was converting to Christianity. Gradlon, for his part, survives because of his Christian faith. The story, therefore, turns on a question of religious adherence. It seems significant that the Númenoreans are the one people of Middle-earth who have anything approaching a religion; by the end of the Third Age it has faded to a mere ritual facing toward the west and sunken Númenor practiced by the Gondorians, as Faramir explains, but Tolkien's *Silmarillion* descriptions of Númenor include the central holy mountain called Meneltarma. As one faction of the the Númenoreans fell under Sauron's sway, Tolkien refers to those who refused to follow him as the Faithful — faithful to their promises, but the capitalization of the word implies a kind of religious faith as well. As in Ys, then, the Númenoreans who are destroyed are the "unfaithful," those who turn their backs on the true faith, and those who survive are the faithful.

Although none of the Celtic legends report the kind of technological mastery that is found in Atlantis (and much of the image of Atlantis as a super-technological civilization comes from nineteenth and twentieth century fantasizers building on relatively small hints in Plato), the fact that these cities and kingdoms are laid on land reclaimed from the ocean, which is held back by dykes, walls, sluices, and other feats of engineering, requires that they be capable of a certain amount of human manipulation of the environment. Inundated lands are always unnatural to some extent.

By placing Númenor and the Undying Lands so close to each other, drowning one and making the other unreachable by run-of-the-mill mortals, Tolkien has conflated the legends of sunken, Otherworldly lands and overseas island Otherworlds from the Celtic tradition with the classical Atlantis tradition to create Númenor. The Númenoreans fall because of the traditional sins of pride and greed; the Elves pass into the unreachable realms, taking much of their wisdom with them. Only a few, Elves or men, are left behind, and the royal line must reestablish itself in new lands.

9. Kings & Heroes

ARAGORN, TRISTAN, & OTHERS

Tolkien narrates *The Lord of the Rings* from multiple points of view: Frodo, Sam, Merry, Pippin, Gimli, Éowyn, Faramir. However, despite multiple shifts in the perceiving intelligence that presents the events of the end of the Third Age, there are really only two "heroes" in the story, Frodo the Ringbearer and Aragorn the King. One is fated to bring the Third Age to its end by destroying the Ring, the other to birth the Fourth Age by reestablishing the Númenorean kingship.

In Frodo, and indeed in all the hobbits, Tolkien created a unique and surprisingly modern race of beings for Middle-earth; Shippey has commented extensively on the "bourgeois" nature of hobbits and their society in both *The Road to Middle-earth* and *J. R. R. Tolkien: Author of the Century*. Aragorn, however, is a very medieval hero: the noble exile, the true heir, the bearer of the legendary sword, the fulfiller of prophecy. (Ironically, the modern hero ends the archaic world and the archaic hero is the harbinger of the new order.) Part of the power of *The Lord of the Rings* derives from Tolkien's contrasting of these two modes of heroism. It is this dual character that makes Tolkien's medieval fantasy accessible to a modern audience in a way that his

Silmarillion tales, narrated from an archaic perception, are not. Once brought into the world of Middle-earth through *The Hobbit* and *The Lord of the Rings*, many readers have the interest to pursue Tolkien's more esoteric narratives, but *The Silmarillion* and other tales of the earlier ages are tough going without that introduction.

One of the many ways of analyzing myth is to look at and compare the underlying structures of a set of myths. Lord Raglan, in his 1936 book *The Hero*, outlined the basic characteristics of the life histories of mythological and legendary heroes by this method, comparing the mythic and epic life stories of a large group of European heroes and extracting a kind of archetypal pattern.

According to Raglan, there are twenty-two archetypal moments in the hero's life: (1) The hero's mother is a royal virgin. (2) His father is a king and (3) often a near relative of the mother, but (4) the circumstances of his conception are unusual, and (5) he is also reputed to be the son of a god. (6) At birth an attempt is made, usually by his father or maternal grandfather, to kill him, but (7) he is spirited away, and (8) reared by foster-parents in a far country. (9) We are told nothing of his childhood, but (10) on reaching manhood he returns or goes to his future kingdom. (11) After a victory over the king and/ or giant, dragon, or wild beast (12) he marries a princess, often the daughter of his predecessor and (13) becomes king. (14) For a time he reigns uneventfully and (15) prescribes laws but (16) later loses favor with the gods and/or his people and (17) is driven from the throne and the city after which (18) he meets with a mysterious death, (19) often at the top of a hill. (20) His children, if any, do not succeed him. (21) His body is not buried, but nevertheless (22) he has one or more holy sepulchers.

The heroes of Western mythology correspond to this scale to rather widely varying degrees. Oedipus is the closest to the archetype, his life containing twenty-one of the twenty-two points; Jesus scores nineteen — as does Dionysus — while the Germanic hero Sigurd scores eleven. Aragorn's life story corresponds with points 1 and 2 (although his parents are not close relatives, and his father is an exiled king); while the circumstances of his conception and birth are not unusual in a mythic way (which tends to involve incest, bestiality, or other violent circumstances), his parents' marriage does come about because of a prophetic insight on the part of his grandmother that his father will not live long, and therefore the couple should marry as soon as possible to be sure of an heir. He is raised in secrecy, but not to hide him from enemies within his family but from his family's age-old enemies; after his father's death in ambush, Elrond Half-Elven becomes his foster-father in a country that is not precisely "far" but certainly alien. His childhood is mostly passed over in Tolkien's relation of the story of Aragorn and Arwen in Appendix A of *The Return of the King*, but on reaching adulthood he begins the enterprise of preparing to reclaim his throne by working against the forces of Sauron. He leads his forces to victory in battle over Sauron (his half of the division of labor between man and hobbit), marries the princess, and becomes king. His reign is marked by peace and the reestablishment of law. It is mostly in the ending of his life that Aragorn departs from Raglan's heroic pattern, for he dies a peaceful, honored death and passes his scepter on to his son. With a bit of stretching, he would get a score of about 13 on Raglan's scale, the same as the English Robin Hood or Greek Pelops.

The relationship between Aragorn and the Arthurian knight Tristan of Lyonesse is not particularly close, but there are a few points of contact that show something of how Tolkien re-imagined traditional themes in making mythology his own. The story of Tristan and Isolde is one of the most famous tragic romances of the Middle Ages, a story about a Cornish hero that is best known in its German telling, although it was also retold in French and English. The legendary Tristan was the nephew of King Mark of Cornwall; he himself was the son of the King of Lyonesse, which sank beneath the waves, according to some versions, at a time when Tristan was off searching for adventure as a young man.

In any case, Tristan was left homeless and dependent upon his uncle, his mother's brother; he became Mark's official champion, the knight who fought in the king's place. As such, Tristan fought the Irish champion Morholt in order to release his uncle from having to pay tribute to the Irish king Anguish. He killed Morholt, but in the process was wounded by a poisoned weapon. Tristan, hiding his identity, was healed by Isolde, a renowned healer and the niece of Morholt. In some versions, he then killed a dragon, was wounded again, and healed once more by Isolde.

The next part of the story varies greatly in the different tellings, but two facts are clear: Isolde hated Tristan because he killed her uncle, and for a variety of reasons, Isolde was meant to marry Mark and Tristan was supposed to escort her from Ireland to Cornwall. En route, the pair accidentally drank a love-potion that was intended for Isolde and Mark on their wedding night and the two antagonists fell fatally in love. For a while they carried out their affair in secret in Mark's court, but eventually they were caught out. In some versions, the couple ran away from the court and lived in the forest, until eventually Isolde returned to Mark out of a sense of her wifely duty, and Tristan went into exile. He found himself in Brittany, where he married a woman also named Isolde, Isolde of the White Hands. Wounded yet again, he sent for his true love Isolde, but, in a Romeo-and-Juliet-ish twist, his wife lied to him about whether the "true" Isolde was coming, and so he died before she arrived to heal him. Isolde, for her part, died when she found Tristan dead.

The story of Tristan and Isolde is a story of adulterous love and ends tragically, while the love of Aragorn and Arwen is almost painful in its propriety and is finally rewarded by lawful union. The points of comparison are small but telling. In many Celtic stories from Britain,

Ireland serves as a kind of rationalized Otherworld, and its inhabitants are endowed with "fairy"-like qualities. Although many elements of the Tristan story vary in its retellings, Isolde is always Irish, and always has the magical power of healing. Arwen, for her part, is an Elf. Therefore, these are both stories that are about the love of a mortal man and an Otherworldly woman. Aragorn and Tristan are both exiled princes who trace their lineage to sunken lands — they are lords of places that no longer exist — and they are in love with women who are explicitly identified as being inappropriate for and unavailable to them.

The medieval romances use this situation as an opportunity for commentary on the morality of courtly and sexual love. Like the love of Lancelot and Guinevere, the love of Tristan and Isolde, for all the emotional (and physical) rapture it creates, is ultimately doomed because of the social responsibilities of the lovers. Isolde and Guinevere are both wives of kings and their lovers are those kings' strongest knights, the kings' champions. Ironically, the champion is the knight who fights in the place of the king so that the king's honor will be upheld without risking the king's life in actual battle. The romances of Tristan and Lancelot serve as a warning as to what could happen if the champion took his role as the king's substitute too literally. There is an implication that, by prudently protecting his life for the purposes of political stability (in the real world, medieval kings who went into battle and got killed tended to leave messy succession problems in their wake), the king risks losing his honor by becoming a *roi faineant*, a feeble, do-nothing king.

Aragorn does not fall into this trap because Tolkien presents him as a king who is his own champion. Tolkien's habit of giving his characters multiple names becomes useful here: If the love of Aragorn and Arwen were to be cast in the mold of the love-triangles of Tristan, Isolde, and Mark, or Lancelot, Guinevere, and Arthur, then it would be a triangle between Aragorn, Arwen, and Elessar, the name that

Aragorn takes when he succeeds to the kingship. Elrond has told Aragorn that he may only marry Arwen when he has reclaimed his throne, essentially telling him that Arwen may marry Elessar but not Aragorn (and certainly not Strider!).

Except for their endings, the stories of Tristan and Aragorn follow similar patterns. The couple first meets under circumstances that bode ill for a relationship — Aragorn is warned off from Arwen by both her father and his mother; Tristan arrives in Ireland with the express purpose of killing Isolde's uncle. Each couple is separated for a while, during which time Aragorn and Tristan both perform more heroic feats, proving themselves heroes. The couple meet again, spend time together, and this time pledge themselves to each other, but it must be a secret, unacknowledged love. This is where the stories part course: Aragorn and Arwen are true to their pledge to wait, while Tristan and Isolde succumb to passion. In some versions of the story, Tristan and Isolde leave Ireland for Cornwall still hating each other, but are tricked into love by the accidental drinking of the love potion; in other stories, they have fallen in love in Ireland and the potion had been intended to cure Isolde of her love for Tristan and transfer it to Mark, her husband-to-be. The potion therefore overwhelms their more spiritual love by swamping it with physical passion.

As a side note, although Aragorn remains true to Arwen, his devotion to her creates the same passionate despair in Éowyn that Tristan's enduring love for Isolde causes in his Breton wife, Isolde of the White Hands; the male lover's loyalty to his inappropriate true love makes him emotionally unavailable to a woman who thinks that she is a better match.

Tristan and Aragorn offer alternate visions of the fate of the exiled prince. Tristan never really settles down — he lives at Mark's court, finds himself in Ireland for a while, returns to Cornwall, flees the court for the forest, is exiled, and winds up in yet another country, where he lives in his wife's court. In most Arthurian stories, a knight spends some time jousting around the countryside, having adventures and proving himself, but ultimately he marries and settles down in his *own* land, having come into his inheritance. There is no inheritance for Tristan to come into, and thus he is rootless as well as landless, and potentially dangerous.

Aragorn is also landless, the king of a country that is currently being ruled by the stewards of his ancestors. Tolkien actually makes a sideways reference to the dangers of the *roi faineant* here in his kings and stewards of Gondor. The most famous example of a kingly line fading into feebleness while their stewards wield the real power and eventually take the throne as well is the case of the Merovingian kings of France — the kings to whom the term *roi faineant* was first applied — and their palace mayors, the family that came to be known as the Carolingians after their most famous son, Charlemagne. The family of Denethor is very much in the same position as those palace mayors, and when they enter *The Lord of the Rings*, they are clearly pondering whether to take that final step to power.

Aragorn evidently returns to claim his throne just in time, for within the family of Denethor the question of continued stewardship is clearly contentious. Denethor proudly claims that his line is so noble that they will remain stewards long after other men would have claimed the throne themselves, but this is in response to Boromir specifically raising the question of why they have not done so; Boromir seems to feel that the stewardship should be over and the house of Denethor should become the kings that they "really" are. Faramir, for his part, accepts the notion of stewardship with a humility that is lacking in Denethor's boast; Denethor's words imply that his willingness to forgo the name of king actually makes him more noble than a real king would be. Given Tolkien's political agenda in Middle-earth, it is hardly a coincidence that, by the end of the War of the Ring, Faramir is the only one still alive: Denethor and Boromir have both fallen victim to their pride and ambition despite their authentically honorable intentions. As with the parallels between Aragorn and Tristan, Tolkien has established a historical precedent for his characters and then taken the plot in a different, contrasting direction.

Tolkien very strongly implies that it is his years "in the wilderness" that made Aragorn a strong king. Throughout Tolkien's fiction, the cardinal sin, the sin that inevitably leads to downfall, is pride. Sauron is proud, as was his master Morgoth, as is Saruman; Denthor's pride leads him to commit suicide, and Éowyn's wounded pride, eating away at her through poisonous insinuations of Wormtongue, nearly leads her to commit the medieval equivalent of "suicide by cop." Even within the Shire, the pride and self-importance of the Sackville-Bagginses leads them to succumb to "Sharkey's" vision of an ordered and financially profitable society, with the result that Lotho is murdered by Wormtongue and Lobelia is imprisoned.

In many of his letters, Tolkien mentioned his respect for the working-class men he met when serving in the army in World War I, the kind of men he memorialized in his depiction of the loyal, stubborn, salt-of-the-earth Sam. Like many of the survivors of that war, Tolkien shared the feeling that its unbelievable carnage was caused by the higher ranks' unfamiliarity with the realities of the battlefield, which led them to make unrealistic and disastrous decisions. Aragorn is, above all things, a leader who not only fights along with his men and knows the realities of the battlefield, but also spent decades learning everything there was to know about his opponent, gathering intelligence, protecting the helpless, fighting against the rising powers of Sauron. He does not ask any of his followers to do anything that he will not do himself.

Perhaps one of the major differences between myths and fairy tales is that myths never end happily ever after. Some of them, it is true, do not really end at all — the narrative consists of a series of episodes that may simply peter out without any real conclusion, as with many Trickster cycles — but when a mythical hero dies, he always goes out in a tangle of betrayal, self-destruction, misunderstanding, or self-sacrifice. The high point of the hero's life comes in the middle of the story, when he has achieved his quest. But then Oedipus discovers that *he* is the cause of Thebes' plague and that he has killed his father and married his mother after all; Arthur is cuckolded by his wife and best friend and killed in battle by his bastard son; no matter what heroic deeds the Norse warriors or their gods may achieve, the world will still end in Ragnarök; Beowulf, who killed Grendel and his mother when he was a young warrior and wound up a king, is killed fighting a dragon — aroused by the theft of a cup from his hoard — abandoned by all his men but one.

Aragorn does not conform to the pattern of the hero's final, tragic death; according to the material Tolkien provided in the Appendices in *The Return of the King*, Aragorn died peacefully after a long life and passed his kingship on to his only son (the advantage of having only one son in such cases is that there is no chance of sibling squabbling over who gets to inherit the throne). However, Tolkien had provided himself with two heroes for his story, and the tragic aspect of the hero's end devolves to Frodo. Returning to Raglan's list of elements in the heroic biography, Frodo conforms to very few. His birth is normal and his parents are neither royal nor supernatural, although they are somewhat unusual for hobbits in having died in a boating accident — hobbits in general being averse to water. As a result, Frodo is raised by first his mother's family, the notoriously eccentric Tooks, and then by Bilbo, conforming to the idea of the hero being raised by foster-parents of some sort. His childhood is otherwise uneventful, until he inherits the Ring and Bag End from Bilbo, conforming to the ninth and tenth points in Raglan's scale. The foe that Frodo defeats is the most evil "king" imaginable, Sauron.

Up to this point, Frodo and Aragorn more or less parallel each other in terms of their conformity to Raglan's heroic biography. It is in the denouement that they more literally divide the heroic characteristics between them: Aragorn marries the princess, becomes king, reigns uneventfully, and prescribes laws; Frodo is the one who loses favor with his people (who never really appreciate the magnitude of his achievement and self-sacrifice in destroying the Ring, preferring the swash-buckling exploits of Merry and Pippin and the common sense of Sam) and meets with a mysterious "death" by leaving Middle-earth for the Grey Havens, so that his body is not buried in his homeland.

Sir James George Frazer, in his famous 1922 study of world mythology, *The Golden Bough*, began from the premise that in primitive society, the king was regarded as a physical representative of the cosmos — a notion we have already encountered in the discussion of the story of Conaire Mór — and when he began to wane in his power and virility, he would be offered as a human sacrifice. Frazer would hold that the reason Raglan's heroic biography always ends in tragedy is that these myths reflect an actual ritual pattern. According to Frazer, the king originally was sacrificed every year and his blood was meant to ensure the fertility of the crops. After a while, as kings began to accrue political as well as ritual function, the annual sacrifice began to seem like something of a waste of talent (taking the idea of "term limits" to an unproductive extreme); the problem was, how to continue to ensure the land's fertility without the king's blood? The solution, according to Frazer, was to substitute someone else for the king, someone who was associated with him by blood or by having ritually taken the king's place by serving as a "temporary king," wearing the king's clothing, or even sleeping with the king's wife/ wives, until he was finally sacrificed. The king continued to rule while his shadow-double died.

The entire epic of *The Lord of the Rings* depicts the parallel paths of its two heroes, Aragorn and Frodo. It could be said that Aragorn follows the political quest while Frodo follows the spiritual quest, although both quests are intimately intertwined. By the end of the Third Age, then, Frodo is already Aragorn's double. (Tolkien makes the argument that Gawain serves as a similar kind of double for King Arthur in *Sir Gawain and the Green Knight*, in a lecture he gave in 1953.) It is fitting that Frodo's ambiguous end, sailing for the Grey Havens beyond the ken of his companions — not tragic in the classic sense but melancholy, terminal, marking the irrevokable end of Elvish presence in Middle-earth — is made possible by Arwen bequeathing to him her own place on that ship so that she might become mortal and remain with her husband. Although departing for the Grey Havens is presented as the road to immortality, in Tolkien's world, immortality is a dubious gift (as will be discussed in greater depth in relation to the Nazgûl). The "gift" of her place in the Undying Lands is therefore both a gift in recognition of Frodo's service in destroying the Ring, but also, in a sense, a punishment for his moment of pride in claiming the Ring as his own.

For his part, Aragorn, like Tristan, can never return to his sunken homeland and can never re-establish the intimate connection between men and Elves that obtained in the mythic time of Númenor — but he can create a new world in which kings die peacefully in bed.

10. Dragon Slayer

BILBO, BEOWULF, SIGURD, & SMAUG

olkien was most famous as a scholar for his work on the Old English poem *Beowulf*. His essay "The Monsters and the Critics," first delivered to the British Academy in 1936, is regarded as a turning-point in *Beowulf* scholarship, encouraging emphasis on the poem's literary merit as well as its value as a document of literary and social history. In this essay, Tolkien takes his peers and predecessors to task for judging *Beowulf* by the yardstick of modern literary expectations, against which the poem, written in another age for an audience that had no familiarity with the narrative conventions of the modern novel, could only fall short. (In light of the direction that medieval studies has taken in the ensuing sixty-five years — much along the lines advocated by Tolkien — the commentary he quotes is somewhat shocking; can these highly regarded scholars have seriously castigated an apple for not displaying the removable rind and interior segmentation of an orange?)

Tolkien argued that the goal of scholars should be to understand what the poem means within its own frame of reference and, in particular, that just because modern literature eschews dragons and ogres, their appearance in a work of Dark Age Northern Europe is not a sign of artistic ineptitude. He made a similar argument about *Sir Gawain and the Green Knight* in his 1953 W. P. Ker Memorial Lecture at the University of Glasgow. He was, in fact, arguing for the kind of cultural relativism in analyzing medieval literature that is the basis of today's multiculturalist approach to literature.

Tolkien was fascinated with dragons since his childhood, and he continued to focus on the roles of dragons in his work on *Beowulf*, Norse mythology, and fairy tales. Although he never says so outright, it seems fairly clear that for him, the presence of dragons — and the quest of the hero to kill the dragon — is the essence of "fantasy," which he defined as the central creative process of fairy tales in his essay "On Fairy Stories" (first presented as a lecture in 1939 and published in 1947).

Tolkien was not alone in regarding dragons as the seminal fairy-tale monster. The Russian folklorist Vladimir Propp, in his *Morphology of the Folktale* (first published in Russian in 1928), through analysis of the body of Russian folktales collected by A. N. Afanás'ev, derived what he considered to be their underlying plot structure, or morphology. The plot pattern that he discovers is essentially the plot of the folk tale that Antti Aarne and Stith Thompson called Tale Type 300, "Dragon Slayer," in their *Types of the Folktale*. For their part, Aarne and Thompson seem to have regarded "Dragon Slayer" as somehow paradigmatic of the fairy tale, since 300 is the first number in the section of the Tale Type Index devoted to the classic *Märchen* or fairy tale. Clearly, there is something archetypal about dragons.

Dragons are found in mythology throughout the world, but their nature varies widely. In Asia, dragons are positive creatures, the mythical ancestors of the Chinese, symbolizing divinity, nobility, wisdom, boldness and heroism. In Western mythologies, these traits are more often associated with the dragon's slayer. In Indo-European mythologies, dragons are chthonic beasts (originating and living within the earth) and are regarded as being related to snakes. Like dwarves, another chthonic race, the dragon is often depicted as a hoarder of the metallic riches of the earth — Tolkien's conflict between dwarves and dragon over the treasure of the Lonely Mountain in *The Hobbit* is a natural antagonism between two types of being who lust for the same thing.

While dragons' greed is an element of folk tradition in Europe, their pride — another characteristic of Tolkien's dragon Smaug — derives from Biblical tradition. In the process of translating the Bible from Hebrew to Greek to Latin, which took place in the Middle Ages, several Hebrew words for prideful monsters were (mis)translated as "dragon." As a result, the slaying or taming of a dragon becomes the quintessential miracle to be performed by a saint. The most famous of these is St. George, who slew the dragon and saved the fair maiden. The story of this originally Greek saint, however, bears a suspicious resemblance to the story of Perseus's rescue of Andromeda from a sea monster — which is a kind of aquatic dragon. (It seems somehow appropriate, given the association of dwarves and dragons in *The Hobbit*, that the gate of Moria in *The Fellowship of the Ring* is guarded by a similar aquatic monster; the recolonization of Moria is presented as having been an act of hubris — pride — on the part of the dwarves.)

Despite their evil reputation, dragons are central to the mythologies of both Celts and Germans. The Welsh flag bears the image of a red dragon because of the story in Geoffrey of Monmouth's *Historia Regum Britanniae*, written in 1136, in which Merlin reveals to the evil King Vortigern that his fortress foundations keep falling down because of battling dragons buried beneath them. When the dragons are uncovered, Merlin interprets the victory of the red dragon over the white dragon to mean that the Welsh will eventually drive the English out of Britain.

In Germanic mythology the Midgard serpent, Jörmungand, was literally the foundation of the world; it encircled Midgard (Middle-earth), the world of humans, taking its tail in its mouth. Jörmungand was especially opposed to the god Thor, and at the end of the world, Ragnarök, it is prophesied that Jörmungand and Thor will battle to their mutual deaths. Beowulf's last, fatal battle is also with a dragon. The most famous Germanic serpent, however, must be Fáfnir, the dragon slain by Sigurd in the *Nibelungenlied*.

Fáfnir is a treasure-hoarding dragon, but the interesting thing about him is that he is originally a human. He turns into a dragon when his greed for Andvari's gold, cursed though it is, causes him to kill his father and betray his brother. (The motif of gold-lust causing a human to turn into a dragon is used by C. S. Lewis in *The Voyage of the Dawn Treader*, when Edmund's greed and grumpiness force the transition; like a more natural snake, Edmund's dragonish exterior has to be shed, layer at a time, until Aslan rips through the scaly armor to reveal the naked boy beneath. This is the kind of allegorical use of mythological motifs that Tolkien so disliked and repudiated in his own work.) Fáfnir is impervious to weapons except for one spot on his (literally) soft underbelly. Sigurd has to dig a trench — with drainage ditches — on the dragon's path to be in the right position to hit that spot and yet evade being drowned in the poison that runs out of the wound, and this technique is not his own idea but is suggested to him partly by his mentor, Regin (Fáfnir's betrayed brother) and partly by an enigmatic figure who turns out to have been Odin. After drinking the dragon's blood and eating a piece of its heart, Sigurd discovers he can understand the language of birds.

There is here an echo of the story of Gwion Bach and Ceridwen; in both stories, the young man is working for an older mentor, doing the grunt work for a project that the older one has been planning for a long time. The older one has set the hero to tend something that is cooking (the cauldron, the dragon's heart) and has left the scene

(Ceridwen is away, Regin is sleeping); in their absence, some kind of hot liquid spurts out of what is being cooked (the drops from the cauldron, the blood from the heart) and falls on the hero's finger. He reflexively puts his finger in his mouth and swallows the liquid, and as a result becomes privy to hidden knowledge (poetic wisdom, the language of birds — both commonly called "song"). The first thing he finds out with this knowledge is that his mentor is going to kill him.

Tolkien's Smaug is a dragon in the pure Germanic cast. Like Fáfnir, he is a gold-hoarder, and he has a soft spot on his belly. He is killed on the wing rather than on the ground, but the existence of the spot is revealed to his slayer by a bird; Bard the Lake Man does not need to ingest anything of the dragon because this understanding of bird-language is an inherited trait that marks him as an aristocrat and the rightful king of the Lake Men. Smaug is also smart and tricky, like Fáfnir. The scene in which he questions Bilbo, on the burglar's second foray into the dragon's lair, recalls the conversation between Fáfnir and Sigurd after Sigurd has stabbed the dragon but before he dies. Especially, Fáfnir wants to know his slayer's name, but at first Sigurd refuses to tell him for fear that Fáfnir will use that knowledge to curse him. Bilbo refuses to name himself for the same reason. Fáfnir warns Sigurd that his gold-hoard will bring bad luck and warns him against the malevolent plans of Regin, a dwarf. Smaug uses the lure of his gold to sew seeds of doubt in Bilbo's mind about the dwarves' true intentions — can they really have meant to pay him his share without considering how he would get it home?

Tolkien also applies a motif from his favorite poem, *Beowulf*, to Smaug. The dragon that harries Beowulf's kingdom is aroused when a thief steals a gold cup from his hoard while he sleeps. Bilbo, likewise, steals a gold cup from Smaug's hoard on his first foray into the cave. This theft causes the dragon to rampage and wreak havoc on people not responsible for the theft. In *Beowulf* the thief is a downtrodden slave fleeing a harsh master, and the dragon takes his revenge on the kingdom of the Geats; in this cultural context, slaves were people from "elsewhere," often the families of enemies taken as loot after battle, and so the slave-thief would be understood to be an alien rather than a Geat. In *The Hobbit*, the thief is a hired hand, of a different race from those who have hired him and who have given him a task that is, on the face of it, beyond his capacity; the dragon's havoc is wreaked on yet a third race, who are barely associated with the enterprise at all. Beowulf, the king of the Geats being harassed by the dragon, kills it; Bard, the true king of the Lake Men who are being harassed by Smaug, kills him.

This parallels between *Beowulf* and *The Hobbit* may explain one of the curious things about the latter story: Why does not Bilbo, the "hero" of the story, kill the dragon? That is what heroes are supposed to do. The whole course of the narrative has illustrated Bilbo's evolution from a fat, smug hobbit who takes care of his creature comforts into a wily traveler who uses his wits to get himself and his friends out of circumstances that he is not big enough or strong enough to overcome by sheer force. Somehow, one would expect that he would cap his evolution to heroism by killing the dragon himself. This appears to be one case where Tolkien was deliberately using an epic plot line that had meaning for him even though it may give his audience some pause.

At the same time, Tolkien appears to have a very different kind of heroism in mind for Bilbo. The Germanic heroes who mess with dragons' gold do not come to good ends; the curse remains. This may be because gold has more than monetary value in these hoards. Dragon hoards have glamour, even charisma. The gold is beautiful in and of itself, symbolizing the life-nurturing warmth of the sun (a precious commodity during Northern winters), echoed in the hair of beautiful women. It arouses lust. Heroes, who live their life on a grand scale because they may lose it at any moment, react to gold with characteristic extravagance. Having slain the dragon and won the gold, Sigurd proceeds to have a completely tragic love life. He now has enormous wealth, good lineage, and prowess in battle, so that he is inveigled, by means of a drink of forgetfulness, into marrying a woman other than the one he loves.

Bilbo is a hero of a very different stripe. Middle-earth is an epic universe whose few urban centers are walled like medieval cities; the only classes appear to be nobles, warriors, farmers, and artisans; no mention is ever made of markets or shops; money per se barely exists outside of the Shire (where is the central government to issue the coinage?). Nonetheless, the Shire, and the hobbits who dwell there, appear to live the lives of nineteenth century English villagers — an idyllic memory of Tolkien's life in Sarehole Mill when his mother was still alive. Bilbo brings a very middle-class mentality to his journey, insisting on a contract before he enters into his engagement as burglar to the dwarves. But his businesslike demeanor, his questions about out-of-pocket expenses notwithstanding, is a facade: As Smaug points out, the most important question of all, how his share of the treasure was to be carried home, was not settled beforehand. (This was a problem that also had not occurred to Sigurd, who barely had enough horses with him to bear away Fáfnir's hoard.)

More than matters of finance, however, Bilbo brings what Shippey describes as a "bourgeois" mentality to the dwarves' quest. The phrase is not used with derogatory intent. Part of the success of *The Hobbit* was a result of mediating the archaic, noble, "high" universe of Middle-earth through the character of a hobbit who viewed it with essentially modern eyes. He manages to negotiate a way out of the impasse existing between dwarves, Elves, and men over the distribution of the dragon's hoard with his "business" skills and the terms of his contract with the dwarves.

It would seem that this bourgeois mentality confers a certain degree of immunity from the madness invoked by gold lust. Bilbo finds himself compelled to pick up the Arkenstone, "drawn by its enchantment" (H, p. 213) when he finds it in the hoard and he appreciates its beauty, but he is soon thinking of it solely in terms of its usefulness in making Thorin see sense. Likewise, while he is dazzled by the hoard, he soon finds himself thinking that all these gold goblets are not much use without something to drink out of them. Tolkien often pointed out in comments about both *The Hobbit* and *The Lord of the Rings* that hobbits had the strength of their weaknesses: Their lack of ambition and imagination makes them practical and, in a pinch, heroic. These are all useful characteristics, but they do not make for a dragon-slayer. That role must be ceded to the noble Bard.

There is an interesting contrast set up between the Lonely Mountain and Moria in terms of dragony guardians. Smaug the Fire-Drake sits on his hoard of gold in the ancient home of dwarves; the Gate of Moria leading to the ancient home of dwarves is guarded by a water monster. The monster that Tolkien describes seems to be something more like a giant squid or octopus — it is tentacled — than a dragon, but traditionally the water monsters of Europe are aquatic versions of terrestrial (or aerial) dragons. The dragons that Merlin uncovers for Vortigern dwell in a man-made pool, for instance. St. Columba is said to have had the first recorded sighting of the Loch Ness monster in the sixth century.

We have already looked at the appearance of the banshee in the medieval Irish tale *Táin Bó Fróech* ("The Cattle-Raid of Fróech"); the grievous injury that nearly kills Fróech was an encounter with some kind of monster that grabs him as he is swimming across a lake, for the second time. Apparently this monster, like Tolkien's Watcher at the Gate, takes his time waking up. It is interesting that there are rarely detailed descriptions of these water monsters — it is as though they represent something so repressed, so deep in the unconscious, so alien to the terrestrial mind, that they cannot be clearly imagined. They are the mythic equivalent of the monsters under the bed.

The airy, fire-breathing dragons like Smaug, however, are more concrete, perhaps because of the medieval fondness for paintings of saints such as St. George fighting them. They are also popular opponents for Arthurian knights such as Tristan — it is while recovering from the dragon's poisonous breath that, in some versions, he and Isolde fall in love. These dragons assumed a characteristic form of a long, lizard-like body with or without legs, wings, and an almost horsey skull. In terms of the traditional associations of the elements, water usually represents the emotions, the unknown, the intrauterine state, while air and fire represent thought, life, culture (well-reflected in Smaug's cultured conversation and cunning mind). What is interesting is that Tolkien has encircled his dwarf-homes, dug deep into the earth, with guardians who represent the opposing elements of air/fire and water.

Furthermore, in the two separate books in which these dragon-monsters appear, each is complemented by the other element: Smaug devastates the lake town of Esgaroth but is finally shot down and dies in the lake in a cloud of steam. The Watcher at the Gate, lurking in the waters at one end of Moria, is counterbalanced by the Balrog fire-demon who falls into the abyss at the other. Fire and water surround the realms of dwarves, and both fire and water are necessary for forging and working metal. In their most positive aspect, dwarves create objects of beauty and the weapons and armor of heroes; when their love of treasure becomes corrupt, its monstrosity materializes as dragons.

Dragons, then, represent the evil aspect of the — literally — lower classes, the ignoble, the crass, the greedy. Their slayers, therefore, must be noble: knights and saints and idealists and Don Quixotes. Bilbo will never be a dragon slayer because he is himself too earthy — hobbits, like dwarves, prefer to live within underground, just not so deep — and his virtues too practical. Yet he is the hero of Tolkien's novel. Throughout his novels, Tolkien seems to say that high deeds, the rise and fall of kingdoms and empires, and the overthrow of evil are stirring sights and make for exciting stories, but to really get the job done, you need a little guy. By framing his story as a version of the Dragon-Slayer folktale, Tolkien once again twists traditional material to his own ideological ends.

11. Man & Beast

BEORN & OTHER SHAPESHIFTERS

In his creation of the Ents, Tolkien explored the potentially fuzzy boundaries between and interrelationships among both the sentient and nonsentient worlds, the herders and herded. Treebeard tells Merry and Pippin that many of his fellow Ents "are growing sleepy, going tree-ish.....Most of the trees are just trees, of course; but many are half awake. Some are quite wide awake, and a few are, well, ah, well getting *Entish*." (TT p. 71)

There is something about the Ents that smacks of animism, the religious belief that all of nature has sentience and spirit. The "sleepiness" of Ents and the "wakefulness" of trees takes on extra significance in light of the Ents' loss of the Entwives. Since sexual reproduction is no longer possible, the only way for new Ents to be created is through the "waking" of trees. (It is significant that in his Middle-earth cosmogony, when describing the creation of the various peoples, Tolkien often uses the term "awakening" to indicate the emergence of a new race. "Waking" trees suggests that a new race is about to appear.)

A different kind of relationship between the human and natural worlds is depicted in the figure of Beorn in *The Hobbit*. Beorn's name, as Shippey notes (*Road*, p. 73), is an Old English word meaning "man" that originally meant "bear." Beorn is a man by day and a bear by night; in his former guise he is a rude but jovial host, in the latter he is the scourge of those who would harm his "people," both human and animal. Thus, Beorn's activities reflect one etymology for the Norse word *berserkr*, "one who wears a bear shirt," that is, a human who puts on a bear's skin, literally or metaphorically, to do battle. (The other etymology translates the word as "bare shirt," meaning that they battle naked, which may sound counterintuitive but is a characteristic actually attributed to both the Germanic and Celtic Iron Age tribes. One rationalization of the practice is that the warrior is so fired up — so berserk — that his adrenaline makes him impervious to his wounds; another is that the warrior has put all his faith in his gods to protect him in battle, and if he is wounded or killed, that is simply the will of the gods.)

Every culture that lives in an area where bears are present regards bears as close relations to humans. For one thing, bears are one of the few nonhuman species capable of standing and even walking upright. This also allows them to use their front paws in a human-like way to pick things up. The mother bear's protective love for her cubs is often seen as the equivalent of human care for children. Since bears are omnivores, they are in competition with humans for food — especially honey, berries, salmon, and moose. However, unlike humans, bears hibernate through the winter, which gives them enormous symbolic value in terms of the cyclical changes of the seasons and the concept of death and rebirth.

The Eurasian brown bear (*Ursus arctos*), the type of bear that would be familiar to Northern Europeans, ranges in height from 4 to 7 feet and in weight from 300 to 550 pounds. This gives the animal a height range that roughly equals that of adult humans, from their smallest, on one end of the scale, to giants on the other. In weight, however, the bear is much heavier, nearly all of it powerful muscle. Thus, it is easy to see how the bear would come to be seen as a kind of super-man among animals, endowed with enormous strength and courage. The fact that bears, when taken young, can be domesticated and trained only emphasizes the possibility of relationship between the two species.

Bear skulls have been found at sites of Neanderthal occupation dating from the Middle Paleolithic. Since the most recent anthropological research seems to indicate that Neanderthals were not related to modern humans, this would suggest some interaction between bears and man even before we were truly human. One of the most archaic bear cults is believed to have been practiced from the prehistoric era all the way into the early 1930's by the Ainu of Japan. They caught a bear cub and raised it virtually as a human, feeding it human food and even nursing it if it was too young to eat solid food. When the bear was about three years old, it was sacrificed by being shot with ceremonial arrows. The bear was thought to be inhabited by the spirit of a mountain god, Chira-Mante-Kamui, and the death of the bear allowed the god's spirit return to his mountain home. However, this was accomplished by treating the wild animal as human and keeping it in the village, blurring the line between human habitation and the god's (and the bear's) wild mountain home. The Ainu are more closely related to the transpolar peoples of Siberia than to the Japanese, and thus, somewhat more distantly, related to the Lapps of Finland, making a link, odd as it may seem, to the Scandinavian mythologies.

A ritual to Artemis, the hunter-goddess of the Greeks, took place at Brauron near Athens. The ritual was connected to the myth of Callisto, one of Artemis's attending nymphs, who became pregnant by Zeus (Artemis's nymphs were supposed to remain virgins like the goddess). Artemis turned Callisto into a bear when the pregnancy became evident, and eventually Callisto and her son Arcas became the constellations of Ursa Major and Ursa Minor — the Great and Little Bears. The ritual at Brauron involved young girls who were dedicated to Artemis and then "played bear," being chased by boys who pretended to hunt them. Some scholars have pointed out that the girls who took part in the ritual then left Artemis's service, marrying and having children as usual. Ritually turning into a bear, therefore, was a kind of rite of passage from childhood to adulthood.

Goddesses were also associated with bears in Celtic religion, although the details of their worship is lost. The statue of Dea Artio, whose name means simply "the bear goddess," found near Berne in Switzerland (Berne being another bear-name), shows the goddess sitting on a bench with a basket of fruit in her lap; she is facing a bear, who is leaning forward toward her on all fours, with its mouth slightly open. There is something about the forward pitch of the bear's stance and angle at which the goddess is leaning away from it in her backless seat that suggests the goddess may be slightly alarmed by the proximity of her animal familiar.

H. R. Ellis Davidson suggests, in *Myths and Symbols in Pagan Europe*, that in northern mythologies the bear symbolized "the lonely champion, fighting in single combat and leading his men" (p. 79). She also points out that in many of the Norse sagas, fighting a bear was a rite of passage for the young hero. This martial symbolism of the bear is reflected in the number of Germanic names with the element *bjorn* ("bear") in them; even the name Beowulf means "bees' wolf," a kenning (metaphorical description used in place of a noun or name) for "bear." Bear names are not found only in Germanic mythologies; the name "Arthur" comes from the same Celtic "bear" word that is found in the name of Dea Artio, as does the name of the Irish hero Art mac Conn.

In the Norse Hrolf Kraki's saga, a character named Biarki (another bear name) sleeps through a battle while some kind of spirit double fights in his place in the shape of a bear. Beorn, for his part, although he appears to have a large band of bear-followers (Gandalf observes the footprints of many bears who had danced outside Beorn's hall the first night the dwarf band slept there), hunts and fights on his own. Gandalf also noted that only one, very large set of bear footprints led away from the dancing place, and when Beorn returns, he has caught a goblin and a warg, questioned, and killed them. At the Battle of the Five Armies, Beorn, again alone, provides the berserk power that turns the tide of battle in favor of the dwarves, men, and Elves.

There is a reference in *The Lord of the Rings* to the death of Beorn and the fact that his son Grimbeorn is the lord of many men. Aragorn, explaining the genealogy of the Rohirrim, mentions that they are related to the Beornings and to the Bardings — the descendants of Bard, who killed Smaug — but it is unclear whether Beorn's "people" are also able to shape-shift into bear form, or if the bears he led in a dance that night were simply animals in his service like those who served at his table.

The term "berserker" implies that putting on some kind of shirt turns the warrior into a bear; likewise, in Scandinavian, German, and Eastern European folk belief, werewolves turn from human to animal by putting on a magical belt. Shape-shifting in both Norse and Celtic mythology is always to some extent associated with warriors. The ability to turn into an animal — a fierce, strong animal — is an advantage in battle, but it also blurs the boundary between animal and human, nature and culture, or, as Claude Lévi-Strauss put it, the raw and the cooked. Thus, although humans are the only species that goes to war, we try to relegate war and aggression symbolically to animals.

Beorn blurs the line between nature and culture in ways beyond his own shape-shifting. Not only can he turn into a bear — a wild animal — but his household is populated by animals that are domesticated in the most literal sense of the word. Horses, ponies, dogs, and sheep perform household tasks such as kindling fires, setting up trestle tables, bringing in platters of food, and serving their guests.

Beorn talks to his animals in their own language, but the language he speaks appears to be understood by all three species, a kind of universal animal tongue. Even his house is located in a liminal zone between the goblins' mountains and the threatening Mirkwood, a spot of domestication between two wild and dangerous places.

At the same time, Beorn and his animals are a different order of being from the eagles who have just saved Gandalf, Bilbo, and the dwarves from the goblin and warg army. Those eagles speak the same language as Bilbo and his friends but form their own, hierarchical society ruled by a lord. Even though they are not shaped like the man-like races of Middle-earth — men, Elves, dwarves, hobbits, goblins/orcs — they seem to constitute a race comparable to them. Beorn, and presumably his Beornings, belong to both and neither of the races of man and bear.

The illustration that Tolkien drew of Beorn's hall in *The Hobbit* shows a long, relatively narrow, wooden hall with two lines of posts holding up the roof; in the middle of the floor is a sunken fire-pit and in the middle of the roof a smoke-hole. There is a trestle table set up — an impermanent piece of furniture that can be put up or broken down as needed — with chunks of unfinished tree-trunk used as seats. Between the row of posts and the outer wall, the floor is slightly raised into a dias. This is where the mattresses are laid and beds made up for Beorn's guests to sleep on. All in all, it is a building in which everything is moveable, depending on the situation, and even so, there is little furniture. It looks very much like an Anglo-Saxon-era hall as far as can be reconstructed through archaeology or from incidental information in literature such as *Beowulf.* It also looks very much like a barn — a type of building that developed from this kind of Dark Age hall. The house itself, therefore, also straddles the boundary between a house for people and a house for animals.

Beorn tells tales of the woods and the wilderness; he is bored by the dwarves' tales of metalwork and jewels. He provides the party with ponies and a horse to carry them as far as Mirkwood and food to sustain them as they pass through it — the food consists of bread, nuts, dried fruit, and honey, and while bread is not exactly bear-food, the nuts, fruit, and honey are. In this way, he prefigures the kind of assistance that Tom Bombadil will offer Frodo and the other hobbits on their journey to Rivendell; Tom Bombadil's house, like Beorn's is situated between a threatening forest and a (potentially) dangerous settlement.

Although Beorn is initially a gruff and suspicious host — Gandalf has to bring the dwarves along a few at a time in the midst of his tale of their adventures, thereby both kindling Beorn's interest and minimizing the size of his party until Beorn's good will has been won — once he has decided to accept them he is a friendly and helpful host. His shape-shifting powers benefit Our Heroes. Other shape-shifters are not so benevolent.

Tolkien's wargs are simply a type of sentient and vicious wolf, often ridden by orcs like horses. The word *wearg*, however, is Old English (cognate with Old Norse *vargr*) and although it is a word for "wolf," its original meaning is "criminal," with connotations of strangling. This is not a particularly wolfish means of killing, but the shape-shifting Odin was known as the "god of the hanged" and was accompanied by two wolves, Freki and Geri, "gluttonous" and "greedy." The Germanic word *wargwolf*, meaning "werewolf," therefore has a much more ominous connotation than merely "man-wolf"; the "man" in question is an outlaw, someone who has committed so heinous a crime that he has been exiled from human society. Germanic wargs are people who also have blurred the boundary between animal and human, nature and culture, but unlike Beorn, they are not jolly woodsmen under their animal skins. Tolkien cannot have been unaware of this meaning when he named his wargs.

In Celtic mythology, warriors are consistently associated with wolves and dogs; the name-element *cu* or *con* means this kind of canine-warrior. Even though names like "Arthur" indicate a tradition of bear-warriors, the symbolism that has survived into the literate era is purely canine. In the Germanic mythologies, however, both bears and wolves are still associated with warriors. In many ways, the two animal-attributes are indistinguishable in battle — the *berserkrs*, whose name indicates bear-ness, are often described as behaving like wolves, howling — but Tolkien appears to have made a categorical distinction between the bear-warrior, Beorn, who is defensive and protective, and the wolf-warrior, the wargs, who are aggressive and destructive. This distinction between the beneficial and destructive sides of the warrior's job is one that can arise more naturally within the context of his Germanic mythological influences.

Tolkien's illustration of Beorn's hall seems to be calculated to evoke Old English or Viking imagery in his readers; the next illustration in *The Hobbit* is the dwelling of the Wood-Elves which, as I have already pointed out, seems to be intended to echo the Irish *sídh* or fairy-mound. There is a parallelism between Germanic and Celtic mythologies here that is also echoed in the comparison between Beorn and Tom Bombadil, both of whom can be seen as Masters of the Forest. Tom's mythological roots are Celtic, and his mastery is over the spirits of the natural world: Old Man Willow, the Barrow-wight, even the environment. The peace that Frodo and his friends feel in Tom's house comes from the sound of rain, the freshness of flowers and rushes, green things. It recalls the nature poetry that the Irish began writing in the early Middle Ages, in which the poet describes the beauty and sometimes also the discomfort of living in the wilderness, beyond civilization.

A fourteenth century poem on the Hill of Howth, translated by Kenneth Jackson in his *Celtic Miscellany* (p. 71), praises "The peak bright-knolled beyond all hills, with its hilltop round and green and rugged; the hill full of swordsmen, full of wild garlic and trees, the many-colored peak, full of beasts, wooded." The focus in these poems is on the landscape, with people and animals merely figures within it. The safety that Beorn's house provides for Bilbo and his friends is protection from hunters — the goblins and wargs who are chasing them — and his house is full, not of plants but of animals.

In many hunting cultures there is a supernatural figure known as the Master of Animals who protects the wild beasts that are hunted by man; he must be propitiated and negotiated with in order for humans to hunt without disrupting the balance of nature. Beorn appears to be a similar kind of figure. Perhaps the difference between Tom Bombadil and Beorn in their relationships to the natural world is that Tom appears to live on the level of the very earth and trees, while Beorn lives on the level of the animals and man-like races, who live *on* rather than *in* the land

By deriving the two similar figures from different strains of mythology, Tolkien seems to be playing with the idea that the Celtic peoples of Britain were the original, chthonic inhabitants of the island, while the Germanic peoples were a later arrival, living on rather than in the land. This chronology is also echoed in the contrast between the (Celtic) Elves and the (Germanic) dwarves, the former arising earlier in the history of the cosmos than the latter, and somewhat more faintly in the contrast between the Númenoreans and the Rohirrim.

Throughout his novels, Tolkien produces pairs and doubles that he proceeds to contrast with each other: the brothers Boromir and Faramir, one of whom succumbs to the temptation of the Ring while the other does not; Théoden and Denethor, elderly rulers whose belief in themselves is sapped by the agents of Sauron, one of whom shakes off his influence, one of whom succumbs; Gandalf and Saruman, the two wizards, one of whom remains true to his calling while the other is corrupted by Sauron; Merry and Pippin, one of whom swears allegiance to Théoden out of love, the other of whom swears allegiance to Denethor out of pride; the list could go on and on. The contrasting influences of Celtic and Germanic mythologies, however, must be added to it to understand Tolkien's literary method.

12. What Have I Got in My Pocket?

Riddles & Prophecy

The episode in *The Hobbit*, in which Bilbo meets Gollum under the Misty Mountains and, by a seeming fluke, picks up the Ring in the dark, is the crucial event leading to the War of the Ring and the end of the Third Age. Tolkien revised this episode after he wrote *The Lord of the Rings* in order to make it conform to the plot that had evolved, but from the very start, the episode involved a riddle contest between Bilbo and the creature who lurked in the darkness.

Bilbo and Gollum ask each other five riddles apiece. Gollum asks the ones whose answers are mountain, wind, dark, fish, and time. Bilbo's are teeth, sun, eggs, "a fish on the table, a man sitting on a stool eating it, and the cat eating the bones" and, of course, "the Ring." Except for "teeth" and "fish/table/stool/man/cat/bones," which are traditional riddles found in English folk tradition, Tolkien himself wrote the riddles, following the style of Old English riddles such as those found in the Exeter Book, a tenth or eleventh century manuscript that also contains many poems. (One of these, *Crist*, was written by Cynewulf, the earliest Old English poet whose name is known, and it is in this poem that the word "éarendel" occurs. Tolkien turned that word into the name of the first king of the Númenoreans who, with a Silmaril bound to the prow of his ship, turned into the Evening Star.)

Old English riddles were poems — some quite long, some only half a dozen lines — that describe an object in elliptical terms, referring metaphorically to what the object does or looks like. Some-times they are written in the first person, ending with "Who am I?" or "Guess my name." One riddle, translated by Craig Williamson in *A Feast of Creatures* (no. 63, p. 125), describes an onion, although the phrasing has a misleadingly human-sacrificial ring:

> A stalk of the living, I nothing said;
> Dumb, stand waiting to join the dead.
> I have risen before and will rise again
> Though plunderers carve and split my skin.
> Bite through my bare body, shear my head,
> Hold me hard in a slicing bed.
> I do not bite man unless he bites me,
> But the number of men who bite is many.

The riddle game that Bilbo and Gollum play is a traditional way of passing the time, a way to while away long winter evenings in the northern latitudes. It is a way to show off one's wit and cleverness, both in setting the riddles and answering them. When the riddle form is as poetic as it is in Old English, people tend to tell traditional riddles rather than make them up themselves, so Bilbo's teeth riddle is not only so old that Gollum calls it a "chestnut," but it occurs in other cultures and languages as well; the Welsh version asks, "What is a row of white cattle and a red bull in the middle?" (Teeth and tongue.) Asking and guessing riddles in this kind of game, then, is a test of memory as well as wit — if you have heard the riddle before, you know the answer; if you have not heard it, you have to figure it out. Either way of coming up with a correct response is a testament to one's mental capacity and cleverness.

The motif of the riddle-contest is found in a number of Old English and Norse texts, including the Old English *Dialogs of Solomon and Saturn*, the Norse *Saga of King Heidrek the Wise*, and the poem *Vafxrúxnismál* in the Poetic Edda. However, the questions posed in these contests are not really riddles per se; the opponents ask each other questions in only the most mildly metaphorical language and the answers arise from the contestants' deep wisdom rather than any particular skill with puzzles.

For instance, in the *Vafxrúxnismál*, Odin asks Vafxrúxnir, "Tell me this one thing if your knowledge is sufficient . . . from where the earth came or the sky above." The response is, "From Ymir's flesh the earth was shaped, and the mountains from his bones; and the sky from the skull of the frost-cold giant, and the sea from his blood." (Carolyne Larrington, trans. *The Poetic Edda*, p. 43) This is straightforward mythological information, the kind of information a poet would need to construct kennings in his poetry; the purpose of the Eddas, after all, is to provide a sort of primer of mythology for the use of poets. Other "riddle" exchanges sound more like catechisms, with the "superior" contestant posing a question in a riddling way so that the other one can prove his own wisdom, kind of like an oral exam.

The purpose of the riddling in these contests is to elicit information from figures well known to be wise: Solomon, Saturn, Odin, an especially wise giant or king. It is an opportunity to show off wisdom rather than cunning. There is nothing tricky about it. However, like the contest between Bilbo and Gollum, the participants ask riddles of each other, with some sort of prize for the one who first stumps the other or, conversely, some kind of unpleasant outcome for the one who is first stumped. A more insidious form of the riddle contest is exemplified by the Greek riddle of the Sphinx, which appears in the myth of Oedipus. The Sphinx — a creature that is neither human nor animal, with the haunches of a lion, the wings of an eagle, and the head and breasts of a woman — demands that each person who passes her lair solve a riddle: "What is it that goes on four legs in the morning, two legs at evening, and three at night?" If the correct answer is not forthcoming, the hapless traveler is gobbled up by the monster. Here, only one participant gets to ask the riddle — which is a real riddle, a verbal puzzle to be solved — and the outcome for the unsuccessful participant is unpleasant indeed. The contest between Bilbo and Gollum is somewhere in between: Bilbo gets a guide if he wins, gets eaten if he does not; Gollum gets a juicy meal if he wins, and merely has to walk down the tunnel if he does not. (Although it is unlikely that Bilbo would have submitted to being eaten without a fight, especially armed as he was with his sword.)

The motif of the riddle contest is incredibly widespread throughout folk literature, showing up in both narrative and song. In folk versions, however, rather than the contest of equals — and the equally wise — found in the literary *Solomon and Saturn* or *Vafxrúxnismál*, folk opponents are generally a figure of authority — a king, bishop, judge, or even the devil — and a woman or a commoner — a shepherd, a farmer, a merchant. The point of the narrative is to show up or outwit the authority figure, proving either that smarty-pants book-learning is not much use in the real world or that authority and wisdom are not necessarily synonymous. These riddles are real verbal puzzles, more along the lines of the Sphinx's riddle.

The ballad "Riddles Wisely Expounded," which is the first ballad in Francis J. Child's collection of *English and Scottish Popular Ballads* and which has many variants, usually contains the following six riddles and answers:

"O what is longer than the way,
Or what is deeper than the sea?
Or what is louder than the horn,
Or what is sharper than a thorn?
Or what is greener than the grass,
Or what is worse than a woman was?"
"O love is longer than the way,
And hell is deeper than the sea.
And thunder is louder than the horn,
And hunger is sharper than a thorn.
And poison is greener than the grass,
And the Devil is worse than woman was."

This contest is usually between a man and a woman — the man asks the riddles, and if the woman can answer them, he will marry her. The structure of these riddles is such that the question is framed as though it were describing a concrete object and the answer turns out to be something incorporeal or elusive. In a way, the contest challenges the stereotypical assumption that women are incapable of abstract thought; the woman proves her marriageability by showing that she can see beyond the concrete.

Other riddle contests are won not by answering the riddles correctly (although keeping the game going by answering correctly is important) but by outlasting the opponent. In some folk tales, a human who is inveigled into a riddle contest with the Devil keeps it going until the sun rises and the Devil has to flee back to Hell. In these examples, the hero wins by relying on the literal application of natural laws and phenomena to overcome the opponent; these natural laws are often the subjects of the riddles themselves in other riddle contests.

Thus, the riddles that Odin asks in the *Vafxrúxnismál* are: Where do the earth and sky come from? Where do the sun and moon come from? Where does day come from? Where do summer and winter come from? Who is the oldest being? Where did he come from? How did he have children without a wife? What is the first thing you remember? Where does the wind come from? Where did the god Njord come from? Where do men fight every day? Why do you know all the fates of the gods? Which men will survive the end of the world? Where will the next sun come from after the end of the world? Where do the Norns come from? Which gods will survive the end of the world? How will Odin die? What did Odin say to Balder before he died? These riddles start by asking how the world began and end by asking how it will end; in between they are concerned with the working of the natural world. As Carolyne Larrington notes in her translation of the *Poetic Edda*, it seems that Odin has come to ask these questions as a roundabout way of discovering his own end, and then quickly brings the contest to a close by asking a question that no one could answer except himself.

Vafxrúxnir's questions to Odin are equally cosmic: What is the name of the horse that brings day? What is the name of the horse that brings night? What is the name of the river that divides the land of the gods from the land of the giants? What is the name of the plain where the last battle — the end of the world — will take place? These riddles are concerned with divisions — between day and night, gods and giants (Vafxrúxnir is himself a giant), between existence and chaos or rather, since Ragnarök will eventually be succeeded by a new world, the division between one world-age and the next. Tolkien makes the authorial comment that Bilbo "knew, of course, that the riddle game was sacred and of immense antiquity, and even wicked creatures were afraid to cheat when they played it." (H, p. 74) The comment does not make much sense in the context of the traditional folk riddles that Bilbo and Gollum have been setting each other, but it does with mythological riddles like Odin's riddles above.

There is another way in which the riddle is sacred, however, whether it is a folk or a mythic contest. These riddles work by describing something in a way that both elucidates and masks its true nature; it creates a state of deliberate ambiguity. In a way, the person who poses the riddle takes something that is whole (for he knows the answer) and unmakes it; his opponent's task is to remake it. However, in the space between the posing of the riddle and its solution, there is a state of chaos, the intellectual equivalent of the time before a Creator gave form to the universe. Thus, answering a riddle is, in a very small way, taking on a kind of cosmogonic role; likewise, posing a riddle is taking on a somewhat annihilative one. Perhaps this is why so many of the riddles that Odin poses to Vafxrúxnir have to do with the boundaries between places and times: Odin breaks down the boundaries by asking the riddle, Vafxrúxnir reestablishes and reaffirms the boundaries by answering. While the contest continues the participants trade the powers of creation and destruction back and forth, but when there is a final stumping, one person has both powers for himself: Odin, or Bilbo.

Then there is the "riddle" of the Gordian knot. Alexander the Great was told that the man who untied the knot would rule the world, so he simply sliced the knot open with his sword. In this case, the "solving" of the riddle comes close to the kind of verbal trickery that underlies the "of no woman born" prophecy in *Macbeth* and the similar prophecy about the Nazgûl king.

Prophecy can be a kind of riddle itself. There is the superficial layer, the words that are used to convey the prophecy or tell the riddle, and then there is the underlying truth, the real meaning of the prophecy or the answer to the riddle. Both riddles and prophecies attempt to hoodwink their audience through deceptive words, playing on multiple meanings or tricky turns of phrase. The most effectively riddling prophecies of all time must be the prophecies of the sixteenth century Frenchman Nostradamus, which are so enigmatic that they can be constantly reinterpreted to refer to whatever event or catastrophe is currently looming.

The link between prophecy and riddle is seen, appropriately enough, in Boromir and Faramir's dream, which leads Boromir to Rivendell in time to participate in the Council of Elrond and to join the Fellowship. In the dream, they hear a voice telling them to look for the "Sword that was broken" in a place called "Imladris," where "counsels" will be delivered regarding "Isildur's Bane" and a "Halfling." (FR p. 259).

The Gondorians do not know what to make of this poem because they do not understand the references in it. All that is clear is that they have to look for something, they have to go somewhere, they have to find something, and something or someone will waken and emerge. The most that they can figure out is that Imladris is the place where Elrond dwells, i.e., Rivendell, and so Boromir comes to Rivendell to see if the key to the rest of the enigma will be revealed to him there. It is: The Sword that was broken is Aragorn's sword, the sword of Elendil that proves Aragorn the heir of the throne of Minas Tirith and Gondor; Isildur's Bane is the Ring; and the Halfling who bears it is the hobbit Frodo. The counsels to which the riddle/prophecy refers is the very council in which Boromir relates the dream, the council in which it is decided that the Ring must be taken to Mount Doom and destroyed. The act of solving the riddle both creates action and sets in motion the events that will fulfill another prophecy, the Return of the King.

Tolkien uses political prophecy as real in *The Lord of the Rings*: Prophecies give authentic and reliable information as to what set of circumstances will obtain when certain events are ready to occur. Aragorn is a man who has been waiting all his life for the time to be right to reclaim his throne. The dream that leads Boromir to seek for the Sword that was broken also leads to the sword being reforged and renamed, indicating that the unfinished business that led to its being broken in the first place — the war against Sauron that began the Third Age — is about to be wound up — leading to the end of the Third Age.

Real political prophecy is somewhat trickier. From the tenth century Welsh poem *Armes Prydain Vawr* ("The Prophecy of Great Britain," which prophesied that the Welsh would unite with the Scots, the Bretons, and the Dublin Norse to drive the Saxons from Britain), to the *Fifteen Signs of Doomsday* (a popular piece of apocalyptic literature in the Middle Ages) to the prophecies of Nostradamus, and into the modern age, political prophecies have tended to work in the same way. A writer at time X would like to incite people to take action so that, with luck, some event — the overthrow of a despot, the end of the world — will take place at, say, time X+10. The writer composes a prophecy that, it is claimed, was actually written at time X-10, in which events of the previous ten years are alluded to, and then makes allusions to things that *should* happen in the next decade. Look! says the writer, everything that the prophecy predicted would happen in the ten years since it was received (because prophecies are always received, never constructed) has happened, so the things it says will happen in the next ten years should happen too!

This kind of political prophecy is the kind of thing that Tolkien was objecting to in the march of Birnam Wood in *Macbeth*; it takes the magic right out of prophecy. Tolkien wanted his prophecies to be sacred riddles that revealed the true, destined order of things once the riddle was solved. It seems somehow fitting that Bilbo picked up the Ring while fumbling in the dark, deep within the bowels of the earth, and used it to win a riddle contest. If riddles have to do with erasing and reaffirming boundaries, the Ring muddies those boundaries by conferring invisibility on its wearer, making the wearer into something like a riddle himself, unseen yet solid. If riddles ultimately have to do with making and unmaking the cosmos, the Ring itself threatens that cosmos more deeply than any riddle, and so it itself must be unmade.

13. Where the Shadows Lie

WASTELANDS

Tolkien mentioned in a number of his letters to admirers that he had created the Shire from the memory of his childhood home at Sarehole Mill. The mill itself fascinated Tolkien and his brother, and the miller and his son loomed large in his memory; they turn up as the Sandymans. A farmer who chased the boys after they picked mushrooms from his fields turns into Farmer Maggot. The local rural dialect called cotton wool "gamgee" and Tolkien used the name for his down-to-earth gardener — and after *The Lord of the Rings* was published received a letter from a man actually named Sam Gamgee.

The Tolkiens lived at Sarehole Mill when Tolkien was between the ages of four and eight, the ages from which a person's earliest clear memories usually date, and it was also the period when Mabel Tolkien was still alive. It was an Edenic childhood memory, a vision of how the world should really be, before all the pain and disillusions of life set in. (It was also the period before the Tolkiens converted to Catholicism, an aspect that Tolkien — and his biographers — tend to gloss over.)

Even in Sarehole, however, change was inevitable: One day an old willow tree that hung over the mill-pond, which Tolkien loved to climb, was cut down; worse, the trunk was just left to lie there, a useless hunk of lumber instead of a living thing.

There are three different wastelands in *The Lord of the Rings*: Mordor, the sterile, tortured desert where Sauron rules; the region around Isengard, which Saruman has begun to turn into his own mini-Mordor; and the Shire upon the hobbits' return, where Saruman has taken up residence as "Sharkey" and continued his destruction of the environment. For Tolkien, wasteland always entailed not only the lack of trees, but the wanton destruction of trees.

The theme of the wasteland is endemic in medieval literature, mostly under the influence of the Grail legends of Arthurian romance. The earliest version is found in Chrétien de Troyes' *Perceval*, written around 1185 (the poem is unfinished, and it is assumed that this is because Chrétien died before he could complete it). Three other writers wrote continuations of Chrétien's poem in French: Gautier de Doulens, Manessier, and Gerbert du Montreuil. Another French writer, Robert de Boron (late twelfth-early thirteenth century), wrote two of his own grail romances, the *Didot-Perceval* and *Joseph d'Arimathie*; there were two other, anonymous French romances, the *Queste del Saint Graal* and *Perlesvaus* (part of the Vulgate cycle written between 1215 and 1235). In German, the grail romance figured in Wolfram von Eschenbach's *Parzifal* (written between 1200 and 1210) and Heinrich von dem Türlin's *Diu Crône* (written around 1220), and in Welsh, it was the romance of *Peredur vab Efrawg* (written sometime before 1300). Although *Peredur* is the latest of the grail romances, it is usually assumed that there is a pre-Christian Celtic myth underlying the whole story, which may have been partially preserved in this Welsh romance.

All of these tales differ in their plots and in their heroes — usually Perceval, but sometimes Galahad and in *Diu Crône* even Gawain.

They even differ in their idea of what the grail is — usually some kind of plate or cup, but in *Parzifal* it seems to be some kind of stone, and in *Pererdur* it is a severed head. Following the work of the mid-twentieth century Arthurian scholar R. S. Loomis, it is generally believed that the grail as a cup is a Christianization of the motif of the cauldron of rebirth (*peir dadeni*) that occurs in Branwen, the Second Branch of the Mabinogi, although this identification fails to account for the romances in which the grail is not a cup.

Where the romances are generally in agreement, however, is that the hero sees the grail in a castle owned by the Fisher King (who so called because the hero first encounters him while he is fishing) which is in the midst of a wasteland. When the hero is some version of Perceval, this king is a relative, although he does not know it at the time. The land is laid to waste because of some sin committed by the Fisher King which resulted in him receiving a wound in his thigh that will not heal. In order for the land to be restored, the hero must ask the king, "Whom does the grail serve?" when the grail (in whatever form) is paraded through the hall during the meal. The first time the hero is at the castle, he refrains from asking any questions, often because he thinks it would be impolite, and as a result he wakes up the next morning to find the castle deserted. Once he has found out what was expected of him, he must undergo further trials until he finally finds his way back to the castle; now he asks the proper question, the king is healed, and the land is restored.

The sexual symbolism underlying this story is fairly obvious, especially since wounds in the "thigh" are often euphemisms for wounds to the genitalia. The Fisher King's impotence and infertility are thus echoed in his land's infertility; this seems to be yet another reflex of the pre-Christian Celtic mythology that connects the fertility of the land with the physical well-being of the king, as has already been discussed. Asking the right question heals both king *and* land. There is an interesting twist in the versions featuring Perceval especially, in that he is usually depicted as a kind of "holy fool;" he is raised by his mother far from the court because she does not want him to become enamored of jousting and tournaments like his father, who died in a tournament. As a result, when Perceval finally does learn about knighthood, he leaves his mother and makes for Arthur's court to become a knight, but since he has noble blood but no noble upbringing, he makes many gaffes and is the epitome of the most *un*courtly knight imaginable. When he arrives at the Fisher King's castle, he has been slowly learning to behave with proper etiquette, and thus he refrains from asking questions because he is afraid to seem rude. (In the Welsh version, there is a wonderful scene where Peredur is being given hospitality at the castle of a one-eyed knight: He gets uproariously drunk and asks his host, "Hey, so who put your eye out?" It does not go over well, illustrating the importance of politeness under most circumstances.) However, the grail procession is a case in which asking questions is necessary, and it seems that the lesson that Perceval is learning is not only how to behave according to the rules of polite society, but also when those rules should be bent.

Perceval is an outsider, someone who is laughed at by the sophisticates at Arthur's court but who ultimately restores the wasteland to life. In this way, he bears some resemblance to Frodo, who is also an outsider, one not used to the high counsels of Elves and men. Each is in some way destined to his role, but each also fails in his quest as well as achieving it. The circumstances are different, with Perceval failing out of ignorance and Frodo out of pride, but for each, their failure is an acknowledgment of powers stronger than they are: They are not superheroes.

Although the Fisher King's wasteland is the most famous — and magical — of the medieval wastelands, the idea of wasteland is found much more broadly. "Wasteland" is a general term for lands that are of no use to humans — they are no good for farming, grazing, hunting, living. Monsters dwell there, and sometimes evil spirits. The terrain that Gawain travels through on his way to meet the Green Knight is wasteland, and there he encounters dragons, wolves, wood-trolls, bulls, bears, boars, and ogres. In the Welsh Arthurian romances, the hero is often said to travel through *eithafoed byt a diffeithwch*, "the limits of the world and its wastelands," before coming on some habitation where he obtains lodging and perhaps information that will aid him in his quest.

Wastelands exist on the boundaries of the human world; castles and towns are oases scattered among the wastelands where landscape is tamed and made fruitful. There is very little sense in most medieval literature of the wilderness as a nurturing place where humans can happily and safely make their home; this image occurs most often in Irish literature and in the romance of Tristan. In Manawydan, the Third Branch of the Mabinogi, a spell much like the curse on the Fisher King's land is laid on the kingdom of Dyfed. As a result of the curse, all humans and domestic animals mysteriously vanish except for the four protagonists, Manawydan, his wife Rhiannon, his stepson Pryderi, and Pryderi's wife Cigfa. Although they manage to live for a few years by hunting wild animals, eventually they decide that they must leave this wasteland and so they move to England, where they engage in various crafts. Humans, the story seems to say, need to live with other humans; the best land is domesticated, and the un-domestication of the land — turning it to wasteland — is a curse.

Although Tolkien uses the idea of wasteland in *The Lord of the Rings* in a way that seems quite mythic and medieval, he actually gives it a very modern spin. For him, wasteland is created by too much human interference, not too little, as the medieval mind would think. This is an attitude that really has to derive from a mind nurtured in the post-Industrial Revolution era. Even more, Tolkien's depiction of Mordor and the lands that surround it can only have come from a writer who survived the trenches of World War I.

Prior to the Industrial Revolution, humans had engaged in activities that caused pollution, but on such a small scale that the effects were not always immediately evident. Even when, for instance, the early Irish effectively deforested the island, or the Maori hunted several species of indigenous bird species to extinction, the changes happened relatively gradually. It was not possible for one person to see a radical change in the environment within the course of a single lifetime, let alone within mere decades.

Furthermore, the effects of pollution were relatively easy to escape: If the side-effects of metallurgy poisoned one location, one simply picked up and moved on. The Industrial Revolution made trends that had been growing slowly over time suddenly accelerate in their effects on the environment. Investment in large factories tied pollution-producers to one location; required a large population of workers who had to live in conditions of unprecedented overcrowding; eliminated the context of traditional, agricultural knowledge and learning without putting anything in its place besides the mechanistic tasks required to work machines; and consumed such large amounts of raw materials that thoughtful conservation was out of the question simply due to lack of time to think about it.

The medieval mind did not generally value the wild landscape because there was too much of it about, and it was threatening to humans. Appreciation of wilderness arises with the Romantic movement in the late eighteenth and early nineteenth centuries, just when the wild was beginning to be endangered by the rise of industrialism. Particulate matter from coal fires, used both to heat houses and drive factory furnaces, was mixing with the notorious London fog to produce poisonous smogs that killed 2,000 Londoners in 1880 and 1,000 in 1892 (the year of Tolkien's birth). Even as late as 1952 (when Tolkien was completing *The Lord of the Rings*), a killer fog in London caused the deaths of an estimated 2,000-4,000 people in the course of a week. The area around Birmingham was known as the "Black Country" because of the soot deposited by coal-burning factories. In 1851 a landowner downstream from the outflow of the public sewer sued the city of Birmingham for making the River Tame unusable for any agricultural activity. The presence of a public sewer was itself an innovation; in the early nineteenth century public sanitation was almost nonexistent and thus disease was rampant in the overcrowded slums.

At the Council of Elrond, Gandalf tells the assembly how he discovered that Saruman had gone over to Sauron's side. When Gandalf refused to join him, Saruman had him imprisoned at the top of Orthanc, from where Gandalf could look over the valley and see the ruin and industrial-like machine works bellowing smoke. Later, Treebeard comments on the constant smoke rising from Orthanc and Saruman's insatiable need for trees to fire his furnaces; even worse, Saruman cuts down good trees and just leaves the trunks to rot — like the willow by the mill-pond of Sarehole Mill. When the Rohirrim arrive at Isengard after the Battle of Helm's Deep, they find that the fortress has been literally undermined with the shafts and tunnels that Saruman has sunk into the earth; the grass has been paved over with stone, the trees replaced with stone and metal pillars and chains; "in the moonlight the Ring of Isengard looked like a graveyard of the unquiet dead." (TT, p. 160)

Isengard represents a different kind of mining community from Moria, and whether intentionally or not, Tolkien seems to represent the beneficial and the destructive aspects of mining in the dwarves versus Saruman. At Rivendell, Glóin tells Frodo of the changes the dwarves have wrought in the Lonely Mountain where Smaug had lurked. The dwarves have created waterways and roads paved with multicolored stone, pillars carved to look like trees, terraces and towers on the mountain, a kind of living sculpture. They have pride in their work. Moria is an entire community built underground, and the dwarves made it beautiful because it was their home and metalworking their love. Saruman's works at Isengard are intended to rip as much out of the earth as quickly as possible, and above ground, it is crowded with dingy buildings that accommodate workers, servants, and slaves. Even in ruins, the halls of Moria are majestic; even at its height, Isengard can be nothing but sordid.

The fact that Saruman sees his devastation of the land of Isengard as a kind of rape is confirmed when the hobbits return to the Shire and see what he has wrought there. He has acted out of revenge to spoil what he knows is dearest to his enemies' hearts, Gandalf's as well as the hobbits'. Old houses have been burned down, ugly new brick buildings have been erected in their place, hobbit-holes have been deserted and their gardens choked with weeds, and worst of all, rows of ancient trees have been wantonly cut down and brick chimneys spew smoke into the sky. The old mill has been replaced with one full of "wheels and outlandish contraptions" (RK, p. 292) and Ted Sandyman now works the mill for Sharkey's men, even though Ted's father used to own and run the place himself. The Shire is overrun with bullies and bureaucrats who have ceased even pretending that their works are useful; they simply create filth for the sake of filth.

This is not the wasteland of the medieval grail romances. It is closer to the hells of Hieronymous Bosch. Medieval wastelands are places forgotten by God; Isengard and the Shire are places that have received too much attention from man. Mordor is a different kind of wasteland: No Man's Land.

As Frodo and Sam, guided by Gollum, approach Mordor, they first pass through the Dead Marshes. They are surrounded by corpse candles, will-o'-the-wisps that will lead the unwary astray, and Sam, falling on his face in the muck, sees the faces of dead warriors from the last war gazing sightlessly up through the ooze. It is a horrible image, a horrible place, and yet it is not the kind of thing that Tolkien had to make up; he only had to remember it. Along the Western Front, where he was stationed in World War I, the war had been fought to such an impasse that the bodies of men who died in the wasteland between the two opposing lines could not be retrieved for months. Many, by default, became buried in the mud, and long after the war was over, their bones continued to surface with every year's plowing. Soldiers marching across those fields found themselves entangled in both barbed wire and the rotting limbs of their former companions.

After the Dead Marshes, Frodo and his companions encounter even worse. The description of the ruined landscape is horrific, bereft of hope or light. This is a scene of desolation that even Mordor itself cannot surpass; even in Mordor, Sam and Frodo find vegetation doggedly growing, twisted and thorny and shriveled, but its buds still opening to some semblance of spring. Mordor is a poisoned land, laid waste by Sauron's evil, but the lands outside of Mordor are the desolate plains made sterile forever by battle and death. The World War I soldiers who served on the Western Front wondered if spring would ever come again. The incessant shelling stripped the leaves from the few trees still standing, grass was trampled into the ever-present mud, and the only thing that changed was the weather — after the freezing, sodden cold of winter, summer brought the smell of decomposing bodies.

Paul Fussell, in *The Great War and Modern Memory*, and Modris Eksteins, in *Rites of Spring: The Great War and the Birth of the Modern Age*, have traced the roots of postwar modernist art and literature in the disillusionment experienced by soldiers who survived the Great War, and Tolkien is generally considered to be one of the few writers who survived the war with his "Victorian" sensibilities intact. Many of the negative reviews that Tolkien received for *The Lord of the Rings* took exception to what was perceived as his old-fashioned and naive glorification of battle. Certainly Tolkien presents the Battle of Pelennor Fields in the heroic mode (although the intercutting of Denethor's madness and suicide with the scenes of battle somewhat undercuts any impression of unadulterated bravado), but such critics seem to have overlooked the real battle in this war: Frodo's quest to destroy the Ring, which takes him through as modernist a wasteland as anything imagined by T. S. Eliot.

Yet Tolkien ends his war by marrying, in a way, the medieval wasteland of the grail romances with the modernist wasteland of the battlefields of World War I and the environmental wreckage of the Industrial Revolution. When Perceval finally makes his way back to the castle of the Fisher King and asks the fated question, the land is restored to its fertility and beauty in one magical instant. Likewise, as soon as Gollum falls into the Crack of Doom with his Precious clutched in his hand, all the works of Sauron crumble and dissolve in an earthy counterpart to the wave that drowned Númenor. On the Field of Cormallon, those battling under Aragorn see the shadow of Sauron literally lift from the land and dissipate into nothingness. The lesser blight of Saruman also dissipates in a haze of shadow and smoke that rises from his body after Wormtongue stabs him. Although the damage to the Shire is not so instantaneously removed, Sam uses the earth from Lothlórien given to him by Galadriel as a kind of Elvish fertilizer to replant where the most beautiful trees had been felled, and by the next spring, the wasteland has been made fruitful once again.

Perhaps where Tolkien failed to be a modernist was in reaching back to the past for a mythic source of renewal rather than looking to the scientific future for the redemption of the earth. But maybe he also realized, even as he was living through the war, that the Wasteland was nothing new.

14. Life Stretched Thin

THE NAZGÛL & THE UNDEAD

The Nazgûl are perhaps the creepiest aspect of *The Lord of the Rings*. Sauron may be the villain and his hungry, lidless eye, when glimpsed through the Palantír, may arouse babbling horror in the unwary, but his incorporeality makes him a somewhat abstract evil. Saruman is tricky and dangerous, his voice seductive, but he arouses anger rather than dread once his artifices are revealed. The Nazgûl terrify for a number of reasons, possibly because their true nature is only gradually revealed. Having been mortal, they are closer in nature to the hobbits — Sauron and Saruman, after all, are Maiar, and therefore of another order of being from the races of Middle-earth.

Thus, the Nazgûl are a constant illustration of the consequences of accepting one of Sauron's rings of power. Bilbo comments to Gandalf, as he is about to leave Bag End for the last time, that he feels stretched thin, "like butter that has been scraped over too much bread." (FR, p. 41) Gandalf ultimately realizes that this is the effect of Bilbo's wearing the Ring, and although the Nazgûls' rings are less powerful than the One Ring, they have been wearing theirs much longer. Their lives have been stretched so thin that they have become undead.

Tolkien makes references to both vampires and werewolves in Middle-earth, although neither appear in *The Lord of the Rings* or *The Hobbit*. Both species seem to have been confined to the First Age, and Sauron at one point even took the shape of both vampire and werewolf. However, these appear to be monsters of a non-traditional variety: The werewolves are regular wolves that have been possessed by evil spirits rather than humans who can metamorphose into wolf-form either at will or at certain periods of the moon's fullness, and the vampires are bats with steel talons, bloodsuckers and shapeshifters but not, evidently, capable of turning humans into their kind. Aside from dragons, Tolkien does not appear to have been particularly interested in the monsters and bogies of traditional lore.

The Nazgûl are not vampires in the traditional folkloric sense, or even in the traditional fictional sense (for the vampires of horror novels and movies are quite different from the vampires of real legend). The vampire of Eastern European legend, as Paul Barber shows in *Vampires, Burial, and Death*, is usually of the peasant rather than the noble class, does not have anything particularly noticeable about the teeth, bites its victims (if it bites at all) in the chest or thorax rather than the jugular, tends to be extremely plump and ruddy-faced (from drinking all that blood) instead of emaciated and pallid, and is generally clad in a shroud rather than a sweeping cape, or indeed in any kind of street attire. The activities of these vampires are varied. Some seem to be more like poltergeists, pinching women's bottoms, knocking things over, and generally causing mischief and disquiet. Some are more like incubi, returning incorporeally from the grave yet somehow capable of wearing their widows out with their sexual attentions. Others seem to have no real consciousness, but are intent on drawing as many as possible of their former loved ones and neighbors into death with them.

The belief that the dead envy the living and wish to take that life is widespread; in historical cases of "vampires," the real culprit for these deaths may be a contagious disease (Michael Bell, in *Food for the Dead*, traces a number of New England vampire legends back to families that were afflicted with tuberculosis) and the "vampire" who is believed to be causing the deaths is simply the first person in the area to have died of it. The problem for these folk vampires is not that they are incapable of really dying, but that they are quite definitively dead — they are still moving around and they want company.

The image of the slender, pale, noble, fanged vampire as sexual predator dates from the Romantic era. In fact, this image of the vampire was based on the archetypal Romantic himself, Lord Byron. "The Vampyre" was written by John Polidori in 1819, Byron's friend and physician, from a fragment written by Byron himself. It concerns one Lord Ruthven, an enigmatic stranger who enters London society and befriends a young man named Aubrey. The people to whom Ruthven lends money come to bad ends, using the money to slide even further into debt, and the women in whom he takes a special interest die mysteriously. As Ruthven and Aubrey travel through Europe, Aubrey begins to realize that something is not right. They are set upon by bandits and Ruthven is mortally wounded, but before he dies he makes Aubrey promise not to reveal anything about him for a year and a day. Ruthven's body is placed in a clearing where the moon will shine on it, and when Aubrey returns to England, the vampire reappears. Taking advantage of Aubrey's promise and subsequent nervous breakdown, Ruthven marries — and murders — Aubrey's sister and then disappears to wreak havoc elsewhere.

This story was something of a nine-day's wonder in Britain, but in France it had a lasting influence on Romantic writing. Novels and plays continued the adventures of Lord Ruthven much the way that Count Dracula continues to return to stage and screen. Throughout the nineteenth century, however, ghosts were the revenants of choice for tales of horror; it was not until Bram Stoker published *Dracula* in 1897 (when Tolkien was five years old) that the vampire began slowly to become the preeminent monster that it is today. However, the vampire's popularity was not spread so much by novels in the first half of the twentieth century as it was in movies and in the pulp fiction magazines, such as *Weird Tales*, which published a melange of horror, science fiction, and fantasy.

Tolkien was notorious for his dislike of modern literature, proclaiming that he read very little of it, but the few journalists to whom he granted interviews, as well as his biographer Humphrey Carpenter, mention that the shelves of his study were crammed with both academic works on Old English linguistics, philology, and science fiction. He very well may have come across modern vampire tales in his leisure reading, or he may have absorbed the popular image from simply living in the twentieth century. Nonetheless, when proclaiming his dislike for "modern literature," Tolkien apparently was using the term in its most academic sense (and why not, since his academic battles revolved around the enmity between "Lang." and "Lit." in the Oxford English faculty).

Carpenter also mentions that one of the things that irritated Tolkien's wife-to-be, Edith, while she was preparing to enter the Catholic Church, was the fact that her fiancé was living it up in Oxford, going to dinner parties, participating in "rags" or practical jokes and misadventures, and going to the movies. Granted, these were the pre-World War I silents, but the chances are that in the days before Tolkien felt obliged to settle into the stereotypical role of the Oxford don in the mid-1920's, he saw at least some of the early vampire movies. Certainly his references to vampires in the shape of bats in the First Age cannot have been derived from folk tradition (where it barely exists), but only from the popular-culture association of vampires with bats that was cemented by Count Dracula and his cinematic descendants.

The Nazgûl are a kind of combination of ghost and vampire, but the balance is definitely tipped toward the latter. In general, they are invisible within their clothes and therefore wrap themselves in vampire-like cloaks and hoods. However, when Frodo puts on the Ring on Weathertop and finally sees them in their true shape, they are tall, almost skeletal figures with piercing, burning eyes in white, bloodless faces. On other occasions their eyes burn red with fury. They are dressed in the garb of warriors and their leader wears a crown. Their very breath — the Black Breath — is poison, causing a paralyzing lassitude in its victims, who toss restlessly, tormented by nightmares, until they finally die. (This illness bears a strong resemblance to Tolkien's experience of trench fever during the Great War.) Dogs bark when the Nazgûl pass and horses shy, so that a special breed must be created to provide them with mounts, and finally Sauron creates for them winged steeds that seem to be a cross between bat, horse, and pterodactyl.

Compare this with the standard movie vampire, the pale-skinned, burning-eyed ancient nobleman with his sweeping cape, whose bite causes his victims to become weak, febrile, and finally to die. In Stoker's novel *Dracula*, Jonathan Harker notes that the Count's breath causes a nausea in him, although it does not seem to smell overtly bad. (Dracula's ability to climb down the walls of his castle head downwards, like a lizard, bears comparison to Gollum's similar talents.)

The one way in which the Nazgûl differ from vampires is that they cannot turn their victims into Ringwraiths like themselves. However, part of their narrative function is to present a warning image of what might happen to Frodo if he were to succumb to the temptation to claim the Ring for himself instead of destroying it. The Nazgûl were once men, kings and sorcerers, corrupted by Sauron when they accepted the nine rings for mortal men. Possession of these rings has prevented them from dying, but not much else. In a way, their function *is* to turn Frodo into a wraith like themselves, for whenever they are around, he is overwhelmed with the temptation to put on the Ring; each time he does so, its power over him becomes stronger. The wound he suffers at their hands, the "bite" of the broken-off end of the Nazgûl's sword that Gandalf finds worming its way from Frodo's shoulder toward his heart, is never truly healed and causes him each year, on the anniversary of its receipt, to drift into a kind of lassitude beset by nightmares. Although Frodo ultimately makes it possible for the Ring to be destroyed, he nonetheless loses his grip on Middle-earth as surely, if not as malevolently, as did the men who became Nazgûl.

The gradual revelation of what the Nazgûl are and what they are capable of is one of Tolkien's most artful narrative devices. They thread through the first book of *The Fellowship of the Ring* like the hiss of a gas leak, with each appearance only increasing their threat. Although Tolkien is forever branded a fantasy writer, his treatment of the Nazgûl outshines the technique of most horror writers.

The Nazgûl first surface when Gandalf reveals the real nature of the Ring to Frodo. Gandalf mentions them as evils from the past who walked long ago and may walk again, but no one can yet say. They are merely examples of the kind of evil that may be reawakening along with Sauron's rising power. The next appearance is merely as an indistinct — but unpleasant — voice offstage, when Frodo overhears Gaffer Gamgee apparently replying to a query about Frodo's where-abouts just as the hobbit is about to step out the door of Bag End for the last time. The day after, as the hobbits are on their way to Buckland, they hear the sound of a horse on the road behind them;

Frodo is overcome with an unreasoning alarm and makes everyone hide off of the road, but he is nonetheless drawn to peek for himself and sees the Black Rider for the first time. The Nazgûl seems to hunt for something — someone — by means of scent, an unnerving image that reduces the hobbits to the level of prey, like the fox being hunted by the hounds. For the first time, Frodo experiences an urge to put on the Ring that seems to come from outside of himself.

The second sight of the Black Rider comes that night, when it is no more than an unsettling shadow under the trees, but this time it begins to creep toward Frodo, again tracing his scent, and again Frodo feels the urge to put on the Ring. This time the Rider is only prevented from finding his prey by the fortunate arrival of a band of Elves. These Elves, however, refuse to tell Frodo exactly what the Black Riders are, although they make it clear that the Riders are dangerous and that the hobbits should leave the Shire as quickly as possible. In this, the ancient, wise Elves fulfill the same role as the old man in horror movies who always warns the hero of unspeakable, enigmatic evil on the way and advises leaving the area immediately, though the hero never follows the advice because he is young and scientific and does not believe in unspeakable, enigmatic evil, the more fool him.

As the Black Riders pursue the hobbits to Bree and beyond, their terrible nature becomes more clear. The hints, whispers, and shadows flitting past the corner of one's eye have taken shape; their menace is no longer potential but real.

From the scene on Weathertop, where the group is attacked by the Nazgûl, the narrative makes an ever-increasing crescendo as the hobbits and Strider race to reach Rivendell before they are hunted down. Mounted on Glorfindel's white horse, Frodo is nearly captured as he races to the ford of the River Bruinen, and the Nazgûl call to him temptingly to come with them to Mordor (like Dracula's brides tempt Jonathan Harker to come to them), but at the last minute they and their steeds are suddenly overwhelmed by the release of a torrent of water down the river engineered, it transpires, by Elrond and Gandalf.

The Nazgûl grow in menace and in substance as the danger of the Ring becomes increasingly clear to Frodo. They begin as a memory of ancient evil, progress to shadows and whispers, but by the end of Book I they are solid figures on horseback that call to Frodo with clear, distinct voices. Even though they are washed away by a cleansing torrent, they will return. Throughout the next several books, they return to the status of rumor and shadow, until they reappear on their new mounts, the pterodactylish winged beasts that carry them through the skies (themselves figures that seem to come out of silent-era stop-action animation films, like *The Lost World,* which came out in 1925, based on Sir Arthur Conan Doyle's fantasy adventure tales). After that episode at the ford, however, the Nazgûl as a group become less important and their leader, the Witch-King of Angmar, takes precedence.

The ambiguous prophecy of the Witch-King's death — or evasion thereof — has already been discussed: He cannot be "hindered" by any living man. This provision is overcome when he is attacked by both a woman and a hobbit, voiding the prophecy on a technicality as all prophecies are voided. The Nazgûl is brought down by Merry's sword cutting his Achilles' tendon (Tolkien does not name it as such, but the elliptical reference to the Greek hero with a single vulnerable spot on his body cannot be coincidence) and by Éowyn hewing off his invisible head. Decapitation, of course, is one of the most efficient ways, in both folk and popular tradition, for laying to rest a vampire, and like a vampire (and like Sauron and Saruman to come), the king of the Nazgûl dissolves into an empty set of armor and a wail dissipating in the wind.

Sauron corrupted the men who became Nazgûl by appealing to their fear of death. The rings he gave them prolong their lives indefinitely, unless they are killed in battle. This infinite life barring accidents is also characteristic of vampires, and within the terms of vampire lore is a state of being "undead:" not living in the breathing, heart-beating sense, but not dead in the flesh-decomposing-in-the-ground sense. Vampires are forever perched in the liminal zone between true life and true death. The Nazgûl inhabit this same territory. Yet the Elves, who are clearly the highest form of intelligence in Middle-earth except for the wizards, regard death as a gift that has been bestowed on men, which allows them to escape from the burden of eternity that the Elves themselves bear.

The idea that eternal life could be a burden is a very modern concept. In eras when the average life expectancy was the age when most modern Americans are just graduating from college, when the revered, wise elders were those who had managed to reach their forties, every year was precious. These were the eras, too, when the emphasis in vampire beliefs was on the way that vampires stole life from the living rather than on the extended "unlife" that the vampire led; in fact, since specific vampire panics were marked by the actions taken by the living to identify and eliminate the vampire, vampires really were not thought of as having an eternity in which to become bored.

The notion that vampires lived eternally, flitting from place to place as the rising death toll made successive neighborhoods too hot for comfort, arises with the literary vampires of the Romantic and post-Romantic ages. This is, perhaps not coincidentally, the same period in which medical technology was advancing at an increasingly rapid rate and standards of living were rising in the industrialized world to allow people to live ever longer lives. It has been commented that the interest in vampires that burgeoned in the late twentieth century had its impetus in the epidemic of AIDS and the psychological resonance of the idea of disease in the blood. Anne Rice's Lestat and his ilk, who begin to find eternity a burden, or television vampires like Joss Whedon's *Angel*, whose immortality increasingly seems like a literal living hell, seem also to echo the contemporary controversies over euthanasia and the medical ability to "unnaturally" prolong life. These issues were just as relevant to the post-World War I generation, when medical technology was advanced enough to save the lives of many soldiers who previously would have died of their wounds, but not yet advanced enough to give them any real life to live with missing limbs and hideous mutilations.

The Nazgûl appear to be one element of *The Lord of the Rings* that Tolkien created from contemporary rather than ancient mythology. He not only uses the characteristics of the pop-culture vampire to arouse dread with his Nazgûl, he also uses the narrative techniques of nineteenth and twentieth century popular literature, horror and ghost stories, to convey and sustain that dread. Although the lack of prominent female characters in Tolkien's work has been commented on by many critics, it somehow seems appropriate that within this very medieval, aristocratic, and mythological narrative, the death of the most modern villain is accomplished by a woman and commoner.

15. New Wine in Old Jugs

MYTH & THE MODERN WORLD

Tolkien's desire to create a "mythology for England" seems rather redundant at first sight. There are plenty of mythologies in Britain: the Celtic mythologies of Wales, Cornwall, and Scotland, the Old English and Middle English myths of heroes such as Beowulf and legends of Arthur and his Knights of the Round Table or of Robin Hood and his Merry Men, the stories of the miraculous doings of native saints, the beliefs and superstitions of uncanny beings from brownies and boggarts to black dogs and banshees.

The problem is that, on closer inspection, these mythologies are either too localized or too universal. The Celtic myths leak out into Ireland and Brittany; the Germanic myths are better preserved in Iceland and Scandinavia; the Arthurian cycle, the very "Matter of Britain," is rooted in Celtic, not English, myth and flourished throughout Europe. Other mythic material is supremely local: Robin Hood sports in Sherwood Forest; the brownie lived at the farm just over the hill; the banshee follows that Irish family who moved in down the street when your grandmother was first married.

The fact that Tolkien was a professor of Old English has misled many people into assuming that any "English" mythology he would construct would be largely based on the Germanic myths that were his main scholarly focus. But Tolkien was interested in all the mythologies current in twentieth century Britain: The Germanic and Celtic mythologies of the oldest literate peoples of the island, whose languages he studied; the high medieval and Christian belief systems; the veneer of classical mythology laid down by post-Enlightenment public school education; and even bits and pieces of the popular mythology of the movies and of science fiction and fantasy. All of them made their way into Middle-earth.

At the same time, while Tolkien clearly was inspired by the many mythologies he studied, he rarely simply repeated his source material with new names and in new environments. Myth was his starting point, but his ending point was his personal vision. Thus, Aragorn is like Tristan, but he follows the moral path and comes to a better end. Birnam Wood may have been soldiers in camouflage, but the Ents march on Isengard with real trees in their wake. The Tuatha Dé Danann live in *Tír fo Tuin*, "the land beneath the waves," the Elves live in the Undying Lands, both to the West.

More subtly, Tolkien marries his Celtic and Germanic inspirations, the two strains of mythology most native to Britain, by pairing and contrasting the figures he derives from them in his fiction: dwarves and Elves, Beorn's hall and the Wood-elves mound, Moria and Lothlórien, Beorn and Tom Bombadil. The place that is the most emotionally authentic in Middle-earth, however, is the Shire, the idealized image of English village life, and the heroes of his stories are the plain, little people of the world. In contrast to the aristocratic milieu of medieval myth, hobbits represent a democratic and relatively egalitarian society.

Tolkien's political vision may be conservative, in that he presents kingship as the most appropriate form of government, but his perfect environment, the Shire, is almost government-free. The Shirrifs keep order with a light hand, but the Mayor is virtually a ceremonial position. Personal freedom and personal responsibility are intimately entwined; if both are present, the world can get along pretty well without much official interference. Pride is the primary sin.

The Hobbit and *The Lord of the Rings* work as epic quests, but are they really a mythology for England? The worldwide popularity of the books, oddly enough, argues that they are not. Although the English-ness of the Shire is self-evident, Middle-earth as a whole is too big for the kind of local immediacy required of myth.

However, Tolkien's opus may well be a candidate for a mythology of the modern age. The Third Age is not literally the era between the two world wars of the twentieth century. Tolkien was right in his insistence that the war of the Ring was not an allegory of World War II. The Ring was not the atomic bomb, Sauron was not Stalin, and the orcs were not Communists. His wastelands, however, are the waste-lands of a postindustrial, not a medieval environment; and his villains perpetrate twentieth century evils. His noble and down-to-earth heroes, however, suggest that while evil's face may change with the times, the qualities that overcome it are eternal.

16. further Reading

following the threads of mythology from Tolkien's work to its inspirations and sources can lead in many directions. What follows are some suggestions for readers whose interest has been sparked by some of the discussion here and would like to learn more.

Tolkien's Own Work

A listing of all of J.R.R. Tolkien's now-published works would be redundant, but here is the original U.S. bibliographic information for the books under discussion here:

The Hobbit, Or, There and Back Again (Boston: Houghton Mifflin, 1937).
The Fellowship of the Ring (Boston: Houghton Mifflin, 1954).
The Two Towers (Boston: Houghton Mifflin, 1954).
The Return of the King (Boston: Houghton Mifflin, 1955).

The twelve volumes edited by Christopher Tolkien under the series title *The History of Middle-earth* (Boston: Houghton Mifflin, 1984-1996) provide annotated drafts of the mass of manuscript still unpublished at the time of Tolkien's death and offer some interesting insight into how his conception of Middle-earth evolved.

Tolkien's most important scholarly essays are collected in *The Monsters and the Critics and Other Essays* (London: HarperCollins, 1990). T. A. Shippey's two books, *The Road to Middle-earth* (Rev. ed. London: HarperCollins, 1992) and *J. R. R. Tolkien: Author of the Century* (Boston: Houghton Mifflin, 2001) are particularly insightful about the relationship of Tolkien's scholarship to his fiction; *The Road to Middle-earth* is especially good on the philological aspect of Tolkien's work. To see how Tolkien himself viewed many of the issues under discussion in this book, see Humphrey Carpenter, ed. *The Letters of J. R. R. Tolkien* (Boston: Houghton Mifflin, 1995).

Jane Chance's *Tolkien's Art: A Mythology for England* (Rev. ed. Lexington: University of Kentucky Press, 2001) and *Lord of the Rings: The Mythology of Power* (Rev. ed. Lexington: University of Kentucky Press, 2001) take a more literary approach to the question of mythology than has been taken here.

Philology & Mythology

J. P. Mallory's *In Search of the Indo-Europeans: Language, Archaeology, and Myth* (New York: Thames and Hudson, 1989) is an excellent introduction for those who wish to enter the maze of historical linguistics. Colin Renfrew's *Archaeology and Language: The Puzzle of Indo-European Origins* (New York: Cambridge University Press, 1987) is rather more specialist, but still interesting. The two-volume *Mythologies*, originally published in French under the editorial direction of Yves Bonnefoy and translated under the direction of Wendy Doniger (Chicago: University of Chicago Press, 1991) is a very scholarly but wide-ranging encyclopedia of world mythology that, unlike many other mythology encyclopedias, covers medieval, early modern, and contemporary mythology as well.

William Doty's *Mythography: The Study of Myths and Rituals* (2d ed. Tuscaloosa: University of Alabama Press, 2000) is a very thorough overview of comparative mythology and the various theories that have been used to interpret it.

Germanic Mythology

The primary sources for Germanic mythology have been translated many times. Carolyne Larrington's translation of *The Poetic Edda* (New York: Oxford University Press, 1996) is very good and provides a helpful introduction and commentary on these often enigmatic poems. Anthony Faulkes's translation of Snorri Sturluson's *Prose Edda* (Rev. ed. Boston: Everyman/Charles E. Tuttle, 1992) is the most readily available complete translation. Seamus Heaney's award-winning translation of *Beowulf* (New York: Farrar, Straus and Giroux, 2000) deserves all the praise that has been heaped on it. Jesse L. Byock's *The Saga of the Volsungs: The Norse Epic of Sigurd the Dragon Slayer* (Berkeley: University of California Press, 1990) is a translation by a renowned Norse scholar and includes a very good introduction.

Craig Williamson's *A Feast of Creatures: Anglo-Saxon Riddle-songs* (Philadelphia: University of Pennsylvania Press, 1982) has translations of the Old English riddles from the Exeter Book and a very enlightening introduction. John Lindow's *Norse Mythology: A Guide to the Gods, Heroes, Rituals, and Beliefs* (New York: Oxford University Press, 2001) is a good handbook, with both overview sections and short, dictionary-type articles on specific aspects of the mythology. Hilda Ellis Davidson's *Myths and Symbols in Pagan Europe* (Syracuse, N.Y.: Syracuse University Press, 1989) and *The Lost Beliefs of Northern Europe* (New York: Routledge, 1993) are particularly helpful in comparing the Germanic and Celtic mythologies, showing points of both similarity and difference.

Celtic Mythology

One of the most useful compendiums of Irish mythology is *Ancient Irish Tales*, edited by Tom Peate Cross and Clark Harris Slover

(Totowa, N.J.: Barnes & Noble, 1969). Jeffrey Gantz's *Early Irish Myths and Sagas* (New York: Penguin, 1982) is less extensive in its coverage but the translations are somewhat more colloquial.

For Welsh myths, Patrick K. Ford's *The Mabinogi and Other Medieval Welsh Tales* (Berkeley: University of California Press, 1977) is superb, and it also contains the rarely translated Taliesin stories and a good translation of *Cad Goddeu*. The translation of *The Mabinogion* by Gwyn Jones and Thomas Jones (Rev. ed. Boston: Everyman/ Charles E. Tuttle, 1973) contains the Welsh Arthurian romances that are lacking in Ford, but does not contain the Taliesin material.

Miranda Green's *Dictionary of Celtic Myth and Legend* (New York: Thames and Hudson, 1992) is a useful dictionary-style reference; Green has written a whole raft of books on Celtic mythology that approach the subject by means of archaeological and art historical evidence. Proinsias Mac Cana's *Celtic Mythology* (Rev. ed. New York: Peter Bedrick, 1985) is a good introductory book, as is Simon James's *The World of the Celts* (New York: Thames and Hudson, 1993). It is somewhat more up-to-date but more archaeological in scope.

Alwyn Rees and Brynley Rees's *Celtic Heritage: Ancient Tradition in Ireland and Wales* (New York: Thames and Hudson, 1963) is a fascinating comparative mythological study. Marie Louise Sjoestedt's *Celtic Gods and Heroes* (New York: Dover, 2000) is a small but insightful analysis. Ann Ross's *Pagan Celtic Britain* (Chicago: Academy, 1997) is one of the standard works on the subject.

Folklore

Medieval Folklore: A Guide to Myths, Legends, Tales, Beliefs, and Customs, edited by Carl Lindahl, John McNamara, and John Lindow (New York: Oxford University Press, 2002) is an encyclopedia-style reference book with articles on all kinds of medieval folklore. Vladimir Propp's *Morphology of the Folktale* (2d ed. Austin: University of Texas Press, 1968) is a classic of folklore scholarship but not for the fainthearted. Albert Lord's *The Singer of Tales* (2d ed. Cambridge, Mass.: Harvard University Press, 2000) is not directly relevant to Tolkien's work but offers a good insight into the relationship between "mythology" and "folklore" and is the classic work on the oral composition of epic.

Paul Barber's *Vampires, Burial, and Death: Folklore and Reality* (New Haven, Conn.: Yale University Press, 1988) is an interesting study of the vampires of folk tradition as opposed to those of popular culture. Jacqueline Simpson and Steven Roud's *Dictionary of English Folklore* (New York: Oxford University Press, 2000) offers a good overview of the kind of folklore that Tolkien felt was not enough to constitute an actual "mythology" for England.

Index

Note: italicized entries denote works of poetry or prose

Myth & Middle-earth is the first in a series of books published by Cold Spring Press devoted to fantasy commentary, criticism, and analysis. We welcome your comments on this and future books in our series.

Cold Spring Press
P.O. Box 284
Cold Spring Harbor, NY 11724
or: Jopenroad@aol.com

About the Author

Leslie Ellen Jones studied folklore and mythology, specializing in Celtic and comparative mythology, at UCLA, receiving her doctorate in 1992. She is an associated scholar with UCLA's Center for Medieval and Rennaissance Studies. She has taught at UCLA and Harvard University, and also wrote and taught an online class on J.R.R. Tolkien for *barnesandnoble.com*.

She has written numerous articles on folklore, mythology, and popular culture, and is the author of a forthcoming Tolkien biography (Greenwood Press, 2003), as well as *Druid Shaman Priest: Metaphors of Celtic Paganism* (Hisarlik Press, 1998) and *Happy Is the Bride the Sun Shines On: Wedding Beliefs, Traditions, and Customs* (Contemporary Books, 1995). She works in academic publishing and lives in Santa Monica, California.